Sharing Destiny

By Taylor Thomas

Second Edition

ISBN 978-1475268195

Table of Contents

Chapter 1: Unexpected Discoveries............................4

Chapter 2: A New Understanding..........................12

Chapter 3: A World Unknown............................26

Chapter 4: Finding The Right Guide.....................32

Chapter 5: Stepping Into A New World................49

Chapter 6: Exploring Their New World...............78

Chapter 7: Unexpected Guests.........................108

Chapter 8: Helping Others Find Their Way...........128

Chapter 9: Getting Reacquainted With Old Friends...........138

Chapter 10: More Friends..............................157

Chapter 11: Excursions Into The Unknown..........................185

Chapter 12: Epilogue...................................211

Chapter 1: Unexpected Discoveries

It was a little past 10PM. Destiny was browsing personal ads on her computer in the study. Her husband Mark was sitting next to her reading along as she selected ads that caught her interest.

Over the past few weeks, they had searched out a number of dating websites online until they came across a site called Adult Friend Finder. This website seemed to cater specifically to the type of "relationship" they were looking for. They had just finished creating an account and were eagerly searching the website for personal ads in their area. The search function had a wide variety of options and although they experimented with different kinds of search criteria, a few of the boxes were always checked the same:

Find a...
Man

...who is seeking
A Woman, A Couple (man and woman)

...and is interested in
1-on-1 Sex

This person's race should be
Black

It was about two months ago when Mark and Destiny had been lying in bed talking one night. They had been comparing the sexual experiences they had and the number of people they had slept with before they eventually met each other when Destiny confessed, "You know, I've never been with a black man before." She paused to see Mark's reaction before continuing, "I always wondered what it would be like." Mark raised his eyebrows inquisitively.

Destiny then added thoughtfully, "I wonder if it is true what they say about them. You know... being very well-endowed?"

Mark immediately chuckled before responding, "Maybe it is true."

He began to imagine a large black man on top of Destiny thrusting a massive black cock deep inside her and Mark was surprised to find he was getting hard.

Mark managed to dismiss the thought but later, after they turned off the lights to go to sleep, he found his mind straying back to that image again. Mark tried to imagine coming home and finding Destiny in bed with a large black man and when he did, instead of feeling rage or jealousy, Mark felt aroused. He even imagined what it would be like to spy on them as they made love and again he got really turned on by the idea.

Eventually, Mark drifted off to sleep. The next morning he had completely forgotten about the strange ideas that kept him up the night before.

The next week they attended a company party hosted by Destiny's employer. Destiny developed training material for a large technology company. There were many people in attendance and most were from branch offices out of state.

Destiny was making her rounds while Mark was talking to one of the Sales guys. Sheri, one of Destiny's co-workers, called out to Destiny to come over. Sheri wanted to introduce Destiny to John, one of the out of state training developers.

What Sheri hadn't known was that over the past couple of years Destiny had spoken to John on the phone several times regarding training matters. John had a deep sexy voice and Destiny always suspected that he was black. Eventually, Destiny was able to verify this when she looked up his profile on the company's intranet, which showed his badge picture. Somehow, over time, their phone conversations and emails had become flirtatious and were regularly filled with sexual innuendos. After awhile, Destiny began to look forward to these calls and emails from John because they added a little excitement to her otherwise dull work day.

Destiny felt the whole thing was harmless as John lived and worked a long ways away from her. Destiny assumed that they would never actually meet in person, which made it somehow safe.

But Destiny hadn't considered that John might be attending this company party even though she knew the company wanted to announce the record sales they had for the year and had paid to fly in many of the employees from the branch offices to celebrate. She had been so busy over the past few days that it just hadn't occurred to her that she might actually have the opportunity to meet John at last.

As she walked over to Sheri, it suddenly dawned on Destiny that the handsome black man standing next to Sheri was in fact John. Destiny recognized his face from his badge picture. She could feel her face begin to flush as she thought *what is he doing here?* She wasn't prepared to meet John face to face – at least not right now. As Destiny got closer she noticed that John was very tall and well built. Destiny tried to regain her composure as John smiled and said, "Hey Destiny. It's great to meet you in person at last."

Sheri was surprised to find out that they already knew each other.

Destiny shook John's hand as she smiled and said, "Yeah. We meet at last." She tried not to think about the many times she had fantasized about meeting John or how she liked to pleasure herself in the bathtub while she imagined feeling him inside of her. Destiny tried to make light talk with John while Sheri watched them interact. Destiny was afraid that Sheri might sense the attraction she had for John. They continued talking for a while and eventually Sheri moved on to another crowd.

With Sheri out of the way, John immediately began to make flirtatious talk with Destiny just like they would do on the phone.

Destiny found herself automatically responding to him with her own suggestive talk and the whole experience seemed much more exciting than their usual encounters on the phone. This time, Destiny realized, they were flirting face to face and something could actually come of it if she wasn't careful.

Destiny's thoughts wandered as she found herself dreaming of John suddenly grabbing her and taking her out of the room; some place private where he could ravish her and she told herself, *if he did, she wouldn't resist. Could she resist?* The thought of his black muscular arms around her suddenly made her wet.

Having all these feelings while she was at her own company's party, surrounded by people she worked with every day and her husband nearby too, just made the feelings more exciting, more intense.

She had fantasized about having sex with other men before but she had never actually cheated on her husband. Yet, the way she felt right now, she knew if John asked her to go back to his room with him, she would find a way to do it. She even had to fight back the urge to ask him where he was staying knowing that the question could actually lead to something she knew she could not do; something she should not do but desperately wanted to do.

Mark had just finished talking to one of the out-of-state sales reps when he decided to get another drink. It was an open bar affair. While he was waiting in line, he noticed Destiny across the room talking with a tall black man. She was smiling and laughing at something he had said. Mark was suddenly reminded of the other night when he laid awake unable to get the image of Destiny doing it with a black man out of his mind. Mark remembered she had said that she always wondered what it would be like to have sex with a black man.

As Mark considered this, he began to see Destiny in a different way. He watched her conversing with this man and he thought, *the way she was smiling and laughing...was she actually flirting with him?*

Mark uncontrollably began to envision this tall black man on top of Destiny thrusting deep and hard inside her as she moaned in ecstasy. His heart began to race and he began to breathe more deeply.

Mark became aware that he was starting to get an erection. He tried to get the images out of his mind; images of this tall muscular black man pounding his wife into submission. Mark moved forward in line but these thoughts kept coming back to him and each time he felt more aroused. He fought an urge to look over again at Destiny and this man standing across the room and when he did, he was rewarded with another visual. *Now he was touching Destiny on the arm, almost caressing her arm.*

This sparked a montage of erotic images in Mark's mind that only further aroused him. Mark had to look away. He was aware that his face felt hot and was probably turning red. Mark began to feel very exposed standing where he was. Mark quickly jumped out of line and headed straight to the men's restroom. Inside, he found the place empty. Mark went directly into an open stall and locked the door behind him.

As Mark sat there on the edge of the toilet trying to get a hold of himself, his thoughts kept turning to Destiny and this man. *What where they doing right now while he was sitting here in the restroom? Maybe they were exchanging numbers?* And this thought sent Mark into a full erection. He couldn't help but to reach for his penis and grabbing it through his pants, he began to stroke it.

He stopped himself, realizing where he was. He had never jerked-off in a bathroom before and the whole idea seemed dirty, naughty and somehow... a turn-on. *What if someone came in?* Getting caught jerking-off in the bathroom by Destiny's co-workers was a humiliating thought. But, he reasoned, he was in a locked stall and no one could see what he was doing even if they did walk in.

His thoughts turned again to Destiny on top of this man's cock, riding him fervently. Mark began to unzip his pants and...

The banter between Destiny and John had cooled down considerably. They were talking more about business issues now. But Destiny found that she was already missing the sexual tension that had been taking place between them just a few moments ago. She thought of ways to bring their conversation back to the naughty.

Before she could stop herself, Destiny found herself asking a leading question,

"So where are you staying in town?" Her heart began to race once again.

John replied, "At the Hilton."

Destiny felt outside of her own body as she heard herself saying the next thing with a devious look on her face,

"Maybe I should stop by later."

Destiny had never cheated on Mark before and was surprised to hear these words coming out of her mouth. She wasn't even sure how she could stop by later but almost as a dare, she felt compelled to say it just to see his reaction. Destiny waited for his response with deep anticipation. Mostly she was hoping he would take it as her just teasing him but a small part of her hoped for the possibility he would take her suggestion seriously and accept her offer.

John was speechless for a moment before he said apologetically,

"That would be nice but my wife and kids may have a problem with that."

He paused for a moment before explaining, "They're staying with me back at the hotel."

The inflection in John's voice said it all to Destiny. He was a happily married man and he would not risk putting his marriage in jeopardy by having an actual affair. Destiny realized he had been bluffing all this time and that he felt embarrassed now that Destiny had actually called his bluff.

Destiny felt relief and disappointment spread over her at the same time. She was surprised the situation wasn't more uncomfortable than it was. Even though John quickly declined her offer, it seemed as though he was the one most embarrassed by her advances because he had been misleading Destiny all this time.

Destiny saved him from further embarrassment by changing the subject back to work. They talked a while longer about work before a fellow co-worker joined in on the conversation. Eventually they parted ways. It was an unceremonious end to what was almost an affair. Rarely would the two make flirting comments to each other over the phone again.

Destiny realized that she had not seen Mark around for a while. She began searching the room for him, pausing occasionally to talk with colleagues she encountered. Finally, her eyes caught him walking towards her. She asked concerned, "Where were you? I looked all over for you."

Mark replied, "In the bathroom."

Destiny noticed a slight mist of sweat on Mark's red face and thought he looked like someone who just finished working out. She looked at him oddly for a moment before dismissing the thought all together.

Chapter 2: A New Understanding

Later that evening as Mark was driving them home, Mark noticed that Destiny seemed lost in her thoughts. Mark found he was lost in his own thoughts as well.

He found that every time he envisioned Destiny bent over in bed getting slammed from behind by that black guy, he could feel his heart begin to race and an erection forming in his pants.

By now, his underwear was wet in spots from all the pre-cum that came with every erection. Mark didn't know why this was making him so turned on and as he thought about it, he couldn't help but to feel a little ashamed of himself. *What kind of guy gets turned on by watching his wife have sex with another man?* He knew that this wasn't the right thing to be turned on by. He wondered, *am I a closet voyeur?* And he began to rationalize what he was feeling by realizing that every man is a voyeur to some extent. Every man who has watched a porno and was turned on by it is, by definition, a voyeur. *But, how many men get turned on by the idea of their wife having sex with another man?* It occurred to Mark that this actually wasn't the first time he felt this way.

Mark recalled a time some years ago before he and Destiny were married.

She was living with him then and they had just thrown a party. Their parties where pretty wild back then and filled with plenty of alcohol. It was late and all their friends except for one had just left.

Mark, feeling very intoxicated, had gone to the bedroom to lie down. Destiny, having more than enough to drink herself, was trying to prepare a bed on the living room couch for their friend who they had convinced to spend the night after having too much to drink.

Destiny had already turned off the lights in the house and Mark could hear her in the living room talking to their friend on the couch. The bedroom door was still open and it sounded to Mark that she was just making sure he was tucked in properly. Destiny was always very good at taking care of people when they had too much to drink. They were talking softly and Mark couldn't hear exactly what they were saying as he lay half conscious in bed. But, at one point he was able to make out Destiny saying,

"No, I can't do that."

She was trying to keep her voice down. A few more muffled words and again Mark heard her gently plead,

"You know I can't do that."

As Mark tried to make out the context of the words, it occurred to him that his friend might be trying to convince Destiny to give him a blowjob or maybe a hand job. Mark thought it wasn't an unreasonable assumption considering their friend was single and Mark was sure he must have at least fantasized about fucking Destiny from time to time, although he would never admit it to him. Also, considering how much he had to drink, it all made sense in Mark's head.

Surprisingly though, Mark didn't feel jealous by his friend's advances towards Destiny, if he was in fact making advances. Mark knew everybody had a lot to drink that night and he found it difficult to hold his friend accountable for his actions at this point. He was a guy after all.

Mark considered getting up to check on things because some part of him told him that was what a good boyfriend should do. But maybe it was the alcohol that dulled his judgment because Mark did not get out of bed. Instead he rationalized that Destiny was more than capable of handling a situation like that on her own and it even seemed like she was handling it.

Mark strained to hear what was going on as he laid there patiently expecting Destiny to come through the door at any moment. As time passed, Mark become more suspicious of the goings-on fueled by what he could hear; or at least what he thought he could hear and even what he couldn't hear. All the while Mark could feel a growing sensation in his groin. He was actually starting to feel aroused by what could be going on in the other room even though he told himself it probably wasn't going on. A few times, Mark thought he could hear the ruffling of blankets and maybe even a soft moaning sound but he wasn't sure. Mark began to stroke his growing erection.

Mark couldn't remember Destiny returning to the room that night or how long he lay their trying to listen before he eventually fell asleep. The next morning he had forgotten the events from the previous night.

It was only a few days later that he was able to recollect the experience. The thought of Destiny performing sexual favors for his friend that night was dimly arousing for a moment but then turned to a creepy feeling. Mark was suddenly sure he didn't secretly desire Destiny to fuck any of his friends. Besides, it probably never happened anyway, he told himself. He probably just imagined the whole thing. And, Mark hadn't thought of it much since then.

But this time was a little different. Mark didn't know this guy. He was a stranger to him. *Did that make all the difference?* Mark considered for a moment the idea of Destiny having sex with another white guy and found it somewhat arousing but not nearly as arousing as seeing her with a big black stud. Mark couldn't understand why this made such a difference to him but as he thought about it further, he realized he didn't just want to see her have sex with any kind of black guy; he wanted to see her being ravished by a large, well-built, extremely self-confident black man with a huge cock. That's what really turned Mark on about this whole thing.

And why a black man?

Was it because black men seemed to be studlier or more confident than a white man? It occurred to Mark that a lot of black men seemed to exude a macho tough guy attitude and when it came

14

to sex, they didn't seem too worried about satisfying the woman. It was almost as if black men knew something about women that white guys didn't, that deep inside every woman was a repressed sexual animal and only black men knew how to bring this side of a woman out.

Mark realized he was unfairly stereotyping black men but certainly there seemed to be a number of black men that reinforced this stereotype. Mark was reminded of the various gangster rap videos in which the black men treated women like dirt and it seemed the women loved them for it. Mark knew this wasn't just in music videos either. It had somehow spread throughout their entire culture.

Mark recognized that a lot of teenage white girls pined away over black rappers and it had not escaped Mark's attention that black boyfriends were highly sought after by white girls when he was in high school. *Did they know something the rest of us didn't? Maybe black men really were well-endowed and maybe… it wasn't just about the size of the cocks either.*

Mark considered all the white boys nowadays who tried to emulate black men in the way they dressed and talked. Despite their efforts, white girls seemed to recognize them as a cheap substitute for the real thing.

It finally dawned on Mark that black men had somehow become the alpha males of society. Black men tended to have a stronger and healthier physique than most white men had and this combined with the sexual confidence they exuded drove women crazy.

Mark also knew that women were biologically drawn to mate with the strongest alpha male in a pack and this helped to explain why so many women were attracted to black men now. Mark also suspected that although white men tended to be more financially successful, the desire to mate for this reason was based on intellectual reasons while the desire for a woman to mate for biological reasons were driven by millions of years of evolution. Mark considered now how the flow of hormones in a young woman would go through the roof as they lusted after these strong, healthy and powerful black men.

Mark thought this could explain why black men seem to have a special power over women. Why they were so sought after by high school girls and why so many women found black men incredibly sexy in general.

Destiny had said, "I always wondered what it would be like to sleep with a black man." And now Mark understood the reason why.

But why did I want to see her having sex with a black man?

Mark imagined watching Destiny bent to the will of a strong black man, conceding to his power, relinquishing all control and direction to him, being completely sexually gratified as he dominated her and then it occurred to Mark… This was a condition that he was unable to put Destiny in himself.

Although Mark tried to imagine taking control and exerting his dominance over Destiny while they were having sex, the thought seemed a little ridiculous to him. It was difficult to imagine Destiny being submissive to him. Mark was not an alpha male, he realized. Nor could he imagine himself becoming one. He always treated Destiny as an equal and that seemed to be one of the main strengths of their relationship.

But when it came to sex, Mark often felt that Destiny was not as sexual as he thought she was capable of. Destiny would achieve orgasm but she never seemed to get worked-up into a sexual frenzy the way Mark longed to see her. Mark knew this was because he was not as much of a stud as she would need him to be in order to get her to that level. *Hadn't she once said to him that she wished he could sometimes just take charge in the bedroom?*

Mark now understood what she meant by that. But Mark was not an alpha male and he probably never would be. Mark had also discovered that the more turned-on she was, the more gratifying their sex life was for him and these two things seemed to put a limit on the intensity of their sex together.

Finally, Mark understood why he was so turned-on by the idea of watching Destiny have sex with a black man. Mark knew that if a strong, alpha male type black stud could get Destiny worked up into a sexual frenzy the way Mark couldn't, then Mark would be able to achieve a greater intensity of sexual gratification himself simply by watching her achieve her full sexual potential.

With a better understanding of why he was feeling this way, Mark gradually began to put away the shame he was feeling about himself as he began to contemplate ways of overcoming the limits of their sex life.

Finally, Mark made a mental pact with himself that he would find a way to encourage Destiny to pursue a sexual encounter with a dominant black man. *But where do I start?*

As he drove, Mark asked Destiny, "Who was that guy you were talking to?"

"Which guy?" replied Destiny, hoping he wasn't referring to John.

"The black guy."

"Oh, you mean John. He's the training rep for San Diego. Why?" said Destiny suddenly afraid that Mark could see right into her thoughts and the indiscretions she had wanted to commit earlier this evening.

"I was just curious." said Mark.

Neither talked much for the rest of the ride home.

Later that night as they were getting into bed, Mark, still aroused by the evenings events and with a conviction to see it happen for real, sought the courage to bring the subject up again. Finally, he said, "So this John guy, do you know him very well?"

Destiny answered, "I talk to him on the phone sometimes but this is the first time I met him in person. Why do you ask?"

"Do you think he is good looking?" asked Mark.

After a short pause Destiny replied, "He is alright looking. Why, were you jealous?" with a smile.

"No. Not really jealous...."

"Then why do you ask?"

Mark cautiously replied, "I was just thinking about what you said the other night. You know, that you have never been with a black guy before and always wondered what it would be like."

"Yeah, so?" she quickly said, as she tried to produce a convincing smile.

Mark continued hesitantly "...so I was wondering if you were thinking what it would be like to be with him?"

Destiny smiled and said with a teasing voice "Why? Are you going to be jealous every time I talk to a black man from now on?"

Mark's heart was pounding again and he could feel a heat in his groin as he considered his response. Mark feared that his confession could cause Destiny to lose all respect for him if he wasn't careful. Finally, he blurted out, "Actually... I was thinking if you wanted to try sleeping with a black guy I think you should go ahead and try it... Just for the experience. You know?" Mark felt detached from his body. *Did I just say that out loud?* He felt extremely vulnerable as he waited for Destiny to respond.

Destiny was speechless as she thought of the implications of what he just said. She thought skeptically, *why would he say something like that? Is this some kind of test?* While at the same time she also felt a little aroused at the possibility that he was serious. Finally, she asked suspiciously, "And you would be OK with that?"

After a moment Mark answered hesitantly, "Yeah"

Destiny asked, "Why?"

Feeling this could backfire on him, Mark considered retracting his proposal for a moment but then he found himself trying to explain, "I don't know. I was just thinking if you really wanted to try it, you should, just for the experience and... I don't know... it's actually kind of a turn on to me." Now it was all out there and while he awaited Destiny's response, Mark wondered what he would say next if she decided his proposal was repulsing to her.

Destiny was unsure how to respond. *How could her having sex with another man turn HIM on? Doesn't he still want me for himself? Maybe he is having an affair with someone else and is now looking for a way to alleviate his own guilt by giving me permission to screw other guys?* Destiny felt angry at that thought and then something occurred to her. She had read somewhere that some men actually get-off on their wives having sex with other men. They even like to watch them having sex with other men, especially if it's with a black man. It was called Cuckolding, she now remembered. Destiny couldn't understand how guys could get off on watching their wives have sex with another man. *And what is it about a black man?* She thought. She dismissed it at the time as just some weird fetish that some guys had. But now, she began to wonder if Mark had this strange fetish too. *Is he saying that he wants to <u>watch</u> me have sex with another man? A black man?*

Destiny was now seeing a side of Mark she never knew existed and she wasn't sure how she felt about it. She tried to imagine Mark watching her have sex with another man and found she had mixed feelings about it. It seemed kind of creepy but at the same time it was also kind of a turn on.

Destiny realized that she had some pretty kinky fantasies herself that she had never dared to share with Mark. Some of them even had elements of exhibitionism in them. But, she had never considered actually acting out these fantasies in real life. Yet, if she understood what Mark was proposing correctly, it could actually lead to fulfilling some of her own fantasies as well as his.

Destiny was a fiercely independent woman who liked to always be in control of her life but she was not always like that, she remembered. Destiny could remember past relationships she had with men that were too overbearing for her and some were even abusive. They had insisted on making decisions for her with the expectation that she should just do as she is told and not question her man. And if she did question them, she would often be punished for it later. She learned to resent these kinds of men over time.

These relationships never worked out for long and each time they ended, she found herself gravitating more towards men that were easy going and were more likely to treat her as an equal in the relationship. She had found these types of relationships lasted much longer and this was how she had ended up with Mark.

However, Destiny had only recently discovered that her best memories of sex came from these turbulent relationships she had with overbearing and even abusive men, especially when she was very young. She remembered that although she spent most of her time living in fear while she was in these relationships and had to work hard just to get out of them, they were also filled with some of the most fulfilling sex she could remember.

She remembered the times when she was able to surrender her inhibitions and let her man take charge of her. She remembered that sex was so much more fulfilling when she was forced to submit to her mans every sexual desire. Destiny came to realize that when she was very young, she had somehow learned to get off when men used and abused her in the bedroom and now, even though she was much more mature, she often found herself wishing she could experience that kind of sex again.

Destiny had even tried to recreate this aspect in her relationship with Mark. To relinquish her need to control the situation and let Mark take charge while they were having sex.

However, she found disappointingly, that she just couldn't get Mark to take charge the way she wanted him to - *needed him to*. She discovered it wasn't in Mark's nature to dominate a woman in bed. She thought it ironic that the very thing she found so endearing in Mark, treating her as an equal in the relationship, also made it impossible for her to experience the kind of sex she secretly wanted to have again.

But Destiny had no desire to return to the old failed relationships of her past so Destiny had resigned herself to the fact that she would not be experiencing sex like that ever again. She told herself it was a fair compromise for what she had with Mark and accepted it. And sex with Mark wasn't bad by any means. It was just... not as intense, she thought.

But now, she realized, there might be an opportunity to experience that kind of sex once again. If Mark was serious about letting her sleep with another man, then she might find a man that could dominate her in bed the same way her old boyfriends use to. And maybe Mark will let her sleep with another man more than once, maybe even periodically.

Destiny realized that this may be an opportunity to enjoy the best of both worlds, the loving sustainable relationship she enjoyed with Mark combined with a strong black man to occasionally dominate her in bed the way she longed to be dominated. She thought this was, in a way, like getting permission from your spouse to cheat. But she realized it wasn't cheating if this is what Mark wanted, too. Destiny's heart raced with excitement and passion as she considered the possibilities.

Finally, Destiny decided to put her theory that Mark wanted to be cuckolded to the test. She said, "Well maybe I should try it. I mean if you're OK with it."

Mark acknowledged, "Uh huh."

And after a moment Destiny added, "Maybe you could even watch me doing it with him."

Destiny could see Mark's pupils dilating and his face was beginning to turn red. He was clearly getting excited over her suggestion, which gave her the confirmation she was looking for. Destiny was beginning to find it strangely arousing that Mark wanted to watch her doing it with another man.

Mark's heart raced with adrenaline and he hoped she wasn't just teasing him. Mostly, Mark was just relieved that she wasn't outright rejecting his proposal.

Feeling a little more comfortable now, Mark passively offered, "Yeah, I could do that. I mean just for the experience," which Mark realized was an understatement. If she asked, Mark would have been willing to do just about anything right now to see a large black stud on top of her.

Destiny said teasingly, "We could try it... Just for the experience."

Mark was relieved that she was receptive to his proposal and even a little surprised that she was already OK with the idea of letting him watch her doing it with another guy. Finally, Mark said, "Do you think this guy John would be interested?"

Destiny smiled. She knew that there was no possibility of doing this with John and she didn't want to have to explain to Mark what had happened earlier this evening. Instead, she just said with finality, "No, I don't think he would. Besides, I don't want to try this with someone I have to work with anyway."

Mark could see the potential problems with propositioning someone she worked with but he still felt a little disappointed, as this was the man he had been fantasizing about with Destiny the whole evening. Realizing that they didn't know many black men (really none), Mark suggested another idea, "Maybe we should place a personal ad online."

Destiny knew of a few men that she had always been interested in having sex with and now that seemed to be a real possibility that

Mark had put on the table but aside from John, none of them were black. Destiny ventured to ask, "Does he have to be black?"

Mark wasn't sure how to answer. He tried to imagine himself watching Destiny doing it with a white guy and just like before, it was kind of arousing but it didn't seem as much of a turn on as when he imagined her with a well-endowed black guy. Mark wondered if they had the same thing in mind after all. Confused, he said, "I thought that was the whole point. That you want to know what it is like to sleep with a black guy."

Destiny was turned on by the idea of having sex with a black guy but right now she was more interested in making sure they could find someone who would be able to dominate her in bed. Whether he is black or white didn't really matter that much to her. She could tell it mattered to Mark though. Finally, she said, "Yeah. I do, it's just there aren't many black guys around here and I am not sure we will find one that will be interested in this kind of thing, especially if you expect him to let you watch us doing it."

Mark appeared thoughtful for a moment before saying, "I'm sure we can find someone. Maybe on a swingers website?"

Destiny replied skeptically, "Maybe."

Destiny tried to be more optimistic as she added, "Well, how do we want to write this ad anyway?"

Destiny continued in a sarcastic voice, "White couple in search of black man who is strong and well-endowed to dominate wife while husband watches?"

Mark was turned on by Destiny's decision to use the words 'dominate wife' in her sentence. Maybe they had the same thing in mind after all. He said, "That works."

They talked about it for a while longer but then it was getting late and both of them were tired. The conversation ended with Destiny saying, "So then tomorrow after work we'll see if we can find a website to place an ad on. OK?"

"Sounds good to me," replied Mark. He was glad that she was receptive to his proposition but he had no idea that she would be so enthusiastic about it. It almost seemed like this was really her idea and not his and somehow this notion really turned Mark on.

As they both lay in bed, deep in their own thoughts about how this would turn out, Mark began to caress Destiny's back. After a few minutes, Destiny rolled over and embraced Mark. They made love into the early morning hours. All the while Mark couldn't stop thinking about a tall, masculine black stud mounting Destiny in their bed. Mark even started imagining it was a black stud on top of Destiny thrusting his big cock deep inside her instead of him. He watched her moaning in pleasure and he came.

Chapter 3: A World Unknown

Destiny said excitedly to Mark, "How about this one?"

Mark was sitting next to Destiny by the computer while she browsed personal ads and he worked on repairing a leather corset Destiny had bought a couple of weeks ago. It was already showing signs of wear.

It had been almost two months since that night Mark and Destiny agreed to seek an encounter with a black man and they had both changed a lot since then.

What had started out only as a casual agreement to try something new had already turned into a full-blown obsession for both of them.

Since that night, they discovered that they were not the only couple out there interested in this type of experience.

In fact, once they understood what they were actually looking for and began to use the right search terms, they were astonished to find the Internet was filled with pictures and accounts from other white couples who had recently turned this particular fantasy into a whole new lifestyle for themselves. These pictures also seemed to confirm that a lot of black men were in fact tremendously well endowed. Both Destiny and Mark were shocked at just how big some of these men were.

They searched the Internet with terms like "Interracial Hotwifing" and they found a whole underground community of white couples who were engaging in this new lifestyle. Some of them have been quietly doing it under the radar for many years but most couples had only recently discovered the interracial hotwifing scene.

Mark and Destiny were shocked to read how many white couples were doing it and there was no single answer as to why it was suddenly so popular. These couples offered a variety of different reason as to how and why they got into this new lifestyle and they all seemed to be really enjoying it. Mark and Destiny couldn't help but to feel a little left out of this new underground scene that had somehow really taken off.

They found that while some couples were perfectly content with bringing just one or two well-endowed black studs into their bedrooms, others would go crazy and were always looking for new and bigger black studs to satisfy their insatiable appetites for black cock. These husbands really got-off on watching as their wife's pussy got demolished by one massive black cock after another and the husbands would just beg their wives for more.

Mark and Destiny noticed that these wives, who often described themselves as regular soccer moms and housewives, seemed to be very orthodox and timid beforehand. But, after the first time they gave in to their husband's desire to see them with a black man, it seemed that they couldn't get enough of it as they searched for other black men to fuck with even bigger cocks for even deeper penetration. They seemed to become obsessed with it. Some wives were even engaging in underground gangbang parties with multiple black men at a time. They would let their husbands watch from the sidelines as three, four or even more black studs had their way with the wives. And always, the husbands begged for more.

Mark and Destiny also discovered that to satisfy the growing demand, there seemed to be a plethora of well-endowed single black men who were now making themselves available in online dating communities across the Internet for the express purpose of servicing these married white women while their husbands stood by watching. Sometimes, the husbands would even take care of all the travel arrangements for them.

These black studs were very eager to show up at your home or hotel room and pleasure your hot little white wife. For them, the uncomplicated no-strings-attached arrangement was very appealing.

It also seemed like many of them got-off on the power they had over cuckold husbands while they were forced to stand by and do nothing as their insatiable wives begged them to fuck them harder and harder. Usually, the husband would be forced just to sit in the corner jerking-off as this black man had their way with the wife and then later, the husband would even profusely thank these black men for coming over.

Mark and Destiny even found Mandingo clubs that would periodically throw parties around the country. Many single black studs would attend these parties where white husbands would hand over their wives and the husbands would collectively watch as these studs had an orgy with the wives.

Mark and Destiny reassured each other that they were not interested in making their fantasy into the kind of extreme lifestyle that others had done. They agreed that they just wanted to try it once for the experience but as they continued to read more about the interracial hotwifing scene, they began to secretly fantasize to themselves about engaging in all aspects the lifestyle had to offer though neither of them was ready to confess those secret desires to each other…Yet.

Mark and Destiny hadn't even had their first encounter with a black man yet, but already they were secretly eager to get in on all the action they had read about.

Instead, they agreed to proceed cautiously. They started by placing personal ads on a number of websites seeking a large, well-endowed black man to dominate Destiny as Mark watched.

They waited (with all the other white couples looking for the same) for a response and as they waited for the right man, they went ahead and purchased a number of interracial videos that featured well-endowed black men pounding and stretching the pussies of white women. Both Destiny and Mark were amazed at the enormous cocks these men had and that these women could actually take them all the way inside.

These videos inspired Destiny to purchase a couple of dildos shaped after these black porn stars' cocks. The packaging said they were formed from actual molds of them. One was molded from Lexington Steele and was nine inches long and six and a half inches around!

At first, Destiny had great difficulty getting these enormous replicas to fit into her tight pussy. Mark's penis was tiny in comparison and it took awhile for her to accommodate their thickness and length. What seemed to work the best was for Mark to be on the bed with Destiny while she was on her knees cowgirl style. Mark would support the dildos upright on a tightly rolled up blanket as Destiny straddled the blanket roll and slowly lowered herself onto the dildo. Mark was amazed to see Destiny's pussy being stretched so wide as the black dildo head entered her.

Destiny was skeptical about getting them to fit inside her when she first saw them but she quickly found that once she was able to get over the initial pain of entry, it felt incredibly good. In fact, the deeper she inserted them, the better it felt. It was a mix of pain and pleasure, she thought, and she found it very addicting as they started ordering even larger black dildos for her to play with. Destiny never felt anything quite like this before. None of her previous lovers had been as big as these things were.

Destiny practiced regularly with these dildos. She was eventually able to take one of the dildos all the way inside of her. The sensation initially caused her to gasp in pain (and maybe *pleasure?*) as her reflexes drove her to sit up higher and pull it out a little bit.

Eventually, she found that if she held it all the way in and began to massage her clit, she would have the most incredible series of orgasms one after another for several minutes. She didn't even have to move up and down much. Just resting on it while she played with herself, her body would begin to shudder and her eyes would close as she came again and again.

Watching this, Mark would stroke his cock and erupt all over himself. Still turned on, sometimes he continued to stroke himself and was surprised to find himself cumming again. After what would seem like an eternity for Destiny, the throbbing in her pussy would slowly subside and she felt her whole body relax with the fading of these powerful orgasms.

One night, Mark watched Destiny as she sat on her knees in bed with a dildo inserted all the way inside her. Mark quietly stroked himself in a chair beside the bed, as Destiny appeared to slip into a trance. Destiny was making soft moaning sounds as she sat in this same position for almost half an hour. Much longer than previous times, Mark realized later. Mark was still stroking his cum-laden cock when he noticed that Destiny's body was beginning to sway in an odd way. As Destiny began to fall forward on the bed, Mark suddenly realized she was actually about to faint from the continuous series of orgasms she had just had. Mark reached out to catch her before her face plunged into the pillows in front of her.

Mark was concerned that something might be wrong with her as he tried to shake her back into consciousness. Eventually, she began to come around. She was muttering incoherent words and was unable to support herself as Mark tried to remove the dildo from her and roll her over on to her back. She was very much disorientated for a moment and then finally said, "Wha? What? … What happened?"

She was having difficulty keeping her eyes open as Mark explained to her what had happened. While she tried to absorb this information, Mark suggested that maybe they should call it a night. Destiny agreed without putting up any resistance. Mark pulled the covers up and over Destiny and he stayed beside her as she quickly fell to sleep.

Chapter 4: Finding The Right Guide

Mark looked up from the corset he was working on. Destiny was looking at the profile of an Adult Friend Finder member named 'black_knight215'. On the left side was a picture of him in basketball shorts leaning up against a wall with his arms crossed. All you could see was from the neck down. He wasn't wearing a shirt and Mark marveled at the muscles rippling across his chest.

Obviously, this guy works out a lot, Mark thought as he viewed this muscle bound body clad in dark skin. Below was a thumbnail of another picture. Destiny clicked on it.

It was an up close picture of a massive black cock standing straight out from his groin. Destiny gasped as she slowly said under her breath, "Oh. My. God!" She raised her hand to cover her gaping mouth after she spoke. Her eyes were open wide as she tried to take in this amazing piece of man-art.

Mark tried to estimate its size and thought incredulously, *it must be ten inches long!* More than that, it seemed to have perfect proportions. Mark tried to estimate its thickness, which appeared to be even bigger around than Destiny's Lexington dildo. By comparison, Mark figured this guy was at least twice as thick as he was and almost twice as long. And it seemed rock hard, standing straight out from his body, with only the slightest curve upward. It almost reminded Mark of a very large banana only a little straighter, black and ... perfect.

Finally, Mark said quietly, "Wow," in shocked disbelief.

Destiny, eyes still wide-open and speechless, turned her head to Mark.

Mark could see her trying to conceal her excitement and anticipation as she tried to calmly say, "He lives only 28 miles from us Mark."

Mark said anxiously, "What does his profile say?"

They turned back to the monitor and as they read, they caught some details such as 6'3", 210 lbs., athletic, single, etc.

His personal statement read as follows:

"Hey Ladies, Looking for a good time with no attachments? So am I. My work requires me to travel a lot and I don't have the time or interest for anything serious right now. So please, only send me a message if you're looking for a discreet, 1-on-1 encounters. No Bi-men please.

One thing you should know about me. I have a very large "endowment". Although some may admire this, I have found some ladies cannot handle it when it's fully erect. Also, I like to get full penetration so I hope you can handle it ;)"

"Well I like it," said Destiny.

"So do I," responded Mark.

Mark and Destiny already knew what kind of man they were looking for. As they browsed the Internet over the past couple of months, they found websites offering advice from other couples engaged in this lifestyle. One site in particular had an article called the 'MFM (Male-Female-Male) Guide' which seemed to provide a wealth of practical advice for couple's who were interested in pursuing the wife sharing lifestyle in general and they often found themselves referring back to this article for guidance as they pursued this new experience.

Right now, what they were thinking of was the article's advice on how to make sure you choose the right person for your first encounter. Above the obvious physical characteristics, it is also important to select someone who has the right personality. The article goes on to say that this is a common oversight by couple's that are looking for their first encounter. You may be expecting the stud you selected to come in and take charge only to find out he has a very passive personality and your wife will be forced to provide him with encouragement and guidance throughout the whole encounter. Alternately, the person you select may be too aggressive and make you or your wife uncomfortable and not in control. Either of these outcomes could turn your first encounter into a real disappointment.

While they were reading this part of the article, Destiny had taken the opportunity to confess to Mark that for some time, she had been longing for a man who was more aggressive in the bedroom; someone who could take charge; someone who, she said, could leave her feeling 'taken'. Mark wasn't exactly sure what she meant by 'taken' but he did know what she meant by someone more aggressive. It was as Mark had suspected all along, Destiny needed someone more aggressive then he was in the bedroom in order to achieve a higher level of climax. Destiny was surprised to learn that Mark was eager to see her having sex with a more aggressive man.

They both sensed that 'black_knight215' might be the kind of aggressive man they were looking for. Destiny asked, "Should we send him a message?"

Mark was aware that 'black_knight215' hadn't mentioned he was interested in couples. On the other hand, he hadn't said anything against couples. Mark said, "Sure, let's do it."

Destiny, knowing this decision would start them down a path that would be difficult to turn back from, asked Mark, "Are you sure?"

Mark replied with a definitive, "Yes."

They composed the following message to 'black_knight215:

"Hello black_knight215, we really enjoyed reading your profile and would like to get to know more about you with the intention of ultimately meeting you for a discrete, 1-on-1 evening. Attached is a picture I hope you enjoy and we look forward to hearing from you soon."

They hadn't bothered to put any other details about themselves in their message, as he would undoubtedly take a look at their complete profile before he responded back to them. Destiny was reluctant to attach a picture of herself though. She asked, "What if he knows me from somewhere?"

Mark responded with, "How many black guys do you know that are six foot three, 210 pounds and hung like a horse?"

Destiny smiled.

Mark said, "You know if we don't send a picture, he probably won't even respond."

Realizing this to be true, Destiny conceded to attaching a picture.

The picture they had selected was from a set they took a couple of weeks ago in preparation for this time. On that night, Destiny had dressed up wearing a sexy, short, tight and revealing black latex dress she had bought just for this occasion. She was also wearing a garter belt with black stockings and black high heel shoes. Mark noticed she had been buying a lot of sexy clothes lately.

She spent over an hour fixing her hair and putting on makeup. She looked drop-dead gorgeous. The purpose of that night's activities was to take some pictures of Destiny and have them ready to send in response to prospective personal ads. Destiny was always shy about having her picture taken (especially these kinds of pictures). She had complained that she didn't feel sexy enough to pose for pictures, which simply wasn't true. She had been working out a lot more than usual over the past six weeks and Mark could already see the difference. Her body was more toned than it had ever been.

Mark had teased Destiny occasionally that she was trying to get in shape for her eventual encounter with 'Big Daddy'. That was how they referred to this fictitious well-endowed black guy they had yet to meet but was going to be responsible for rocking Destiny's world as Mark watched. That night, Destiny felt sexy and it showed. As

Mark had her lay back on the couch and strike a pose for the camera, she did so with a smile and without hesitation. Mark took a number of pictures of Destiny assuming various poses before handing her a piece of paper with their screen name in large type on it.

Mark had Destiny strike another posse while holding the piece of paper and took a picture. The purpose of this piece of paper with their screen name on it was to prove the legitimacy of the picture. They had learned that some people will use a picture of any random hot woman they downloaded from the internet in their own personal ads just to get responses.

They selected a picture and attached it, and with one more mutual nod, pressed the send button. Now began the waiting game they were all too familiar with. They had responded to a couple of other ads over the past couple of months and never got a response. They knew that some people created personal ads and then stopped checking their accounts after awhile. However, black_knight215's profile showed his "last visit" to the website was within the past week.

They retired to the bedroom and resisted the urge to have sex. Another piece of advice they got from the MFM Guide. It recommended that once you set a date for your first encounter, it is best to try and abstain from having sex with your partner for a few days if not a week or more until that special night. This helps to heighten the sexual tension in anticipation of your first meeting and will help make the encounter every bit as erotic as you had hoped it would be.

The article went on to say that a common mistake of newbie's is to have sex with their partner the night before or worse, just hours before they had a planned encounter. Although it may be tempting to relieve this tension just before your meeting, doing so has caused many couples to find that they had suddenly lost interest in going through with their planned encounter. Some couples that continue to go through with the encounter found the experience to not be as erotic as they hoped for.

Although Mark and Destiny had not actually set a date with anyone yet, they found themselves going through the motions of practicing abstinence after the first personal ad they responded to and it had since become a tradition. However, they both slept restlessly that night.

The next day, Destiny found herself periodically checking her personal email account at work knowing that she would receive a notification if there were any new messages waiting in their AFF account's inbox. Each time she checked, she was disappointed to find no notifications from AFF.

Later that evening, after Destiny finished her workout and Mark was watching TV, she decided to check her personal email again. She was excited to see a message from AFF in her inbox. The subject line said, "New message from 'black_knight215' at Adult Friend Finder." Destiny called to Mark as she began logging into AFF to read it. Mark arrived as she was pulling up their AFF inbox. They clicked on the message and both of them began to read it:

"Got your message. Enjoyed the picture ;) You two have an interesting profile. I have been propositioned by couples before but it's not something I normally go for. However, I am considering your offer and I am interested in learning more. Specifically, I am interested in what level of involvement your husband expects to have. Does he just want to watch or does he expect to participate? Also, I am not Bi and I am not interested if he expects to engage in anything Bisexual. I may be OK with him watching but I am not interested if he intends to give directions or otherwise share his thoughts or opinions while we are engaged in "activities." In fact, I would prefer it if he didn't talk at all. If these conditions are acceptable, then we can talk further about a possible meeting.

-Ty"

Initially, Mark's ego was a little bruised by the way this guy was dictating to Mark what he can or can't do if he should decide to accept their offer. But then he started to find himself getting a little turned-on by the presumptive nature of his response, which was indicative of a man who is used to taking charge and getting what he wants. Mark remembered his profile pictures and suspected that with a body (and cock) like that; this guy probably had a lot of women to choose from. Mark realized that they were pretty lucky he was interested in their proposal in the first place. Mark thought, *this guy sure seems to be cocky and arrogant. But wasn't that the kind of personality they were looking for? Someone domineering who could take charge and dominate Destiny?* It was, Mark realized.

Regarding his "demands", Mark had already committed to Destiny that he intended to just sit there and quietly watch as he had his way with her. Mark began to feel aroused as he imagined this black stud taking charge and putting Mark in his place before he had his way with Destiny. He grinned as he thought to himself, *this stud is starting to look like the perfect man for the job.*

Destiny was having similar thoughts. She could immediately identify with this man just by the way he writes. He reminded her of the kind of aggressive and domineering men she used to date before Mark. As she read, she thought, *wow, this guy doesn't mess around* and when she got to the part where he said he is not interested in Mark sharing his thoughts or opinions while they were engaged in "activities", a shiver ran down her spine as she thought, *this guy really likes to be in charge* and that was exactly what she had been looking for. She knew right then and there that she would be able to surrender herself to this man. *This could be the one,* she thought to herself.

But Destiny was a little concerned about how Mark might be taking all this. This guy didn't seem to hesitate to put Mark in his place and she hoped that his cockiness wasn't too much for Mark to handle. She knew that in order for this to work with this kind of guy, Mark was going to have to accept a subordinate role whenever he was around and let this guy take charge and call all the shots. On top of that, she was also concerned how Mark might really react to seeing another man taking control of her in the way she wanted. Mark had said that he wanted to see her dominated by a black man and that he intended to just sit and watch as this man had his way with her but she still didn't believe that Mark fully understood the kind of domination she was looking for or what she really meant by 'being taken'. Destiny was afraid that if it happened the way she wanted it to, Mark might misunderstand what was going on and try to intervene right at the worst time. She hoped he wouldn't. And she hoped that Mark could handle this guy's cocky attitude to begin with.

Finally, Destiny asked cautiously, "Well, what do you think?"

Mark tried to appear thoughtful for a moment before finally saying matter-of-factly, "He has a lot of conditions..." and paused before continuing, "But I don't see any problems with his conditions. This is what we are looking for. Isn't it?" Mark hoped he didn't seem too anxious to Destiny as he felt an erection forming in his pants.

Destiny nodded and then added, "I think he's perfect myself."

After a moment, Mark finally conceded, "Yeah. I think he is too."

Getting the assurance she needed, Destiny asked, "How should we respond?"

After spending some time talking about it, they put together the following response and sent it:

"Hi Ty,

Thanks you so much for responding to our message. Just for clarification, my husband is not interested in Bi "activities" either. He also assures you and I, that he only wants to watch and will not be offering any direction or commentary during our "activities." Do you have any other questions for us? Are you still interested? If so, we are anxious to meet you. However, this is our first time and we are not sure how to proceed. Should we talk first? We noticed that AFF has an optional service that allows members to anonymously call each other but we have never used it. Have you? I apologize that we are such amateurs with this and I really hope you are still interested and willing to help guide us through this new experience.

-Mark and Destiny"

As Mark and Destiny sat there, they both were beginning to realize that this could actually happen. Their thoughts alternated between having a case of cold feet and deep anticipation of what was to come. They also knew that if they could maintain their commitment to abstinence, then anticipation would win out over cold feet until they could see this thing through. And they really wanted to see this through.

Finally, Destiny said, "Well, now all we can do is wait," and she promptly got up and left the room. Mark, not knowing what else to add, returned to the TV room.

Again, they slept restlessly that night. Destiny's dreams were filled with all manner of passionate sex as they had been a lot lately. More than once she had to get up and go to the bathroom. There she found her underwear soaking wet and had to change them before returning to bed. Mark dreamed too. His dreams were filled with images of Destiny willingly being taken by various black men while Mark, unable to speak, sat their impotent to do anything about it. He dreamed of these men laughing at his small penis as they had their way with his wife. Mark dreamed of moments of anger that quickly changed to arousal driving him to masturbate as he sat in the corner and watched an endless stream of black men surrounding Destiny; she was touching them as they touched her. Mark dreamed of Destiny getting gang-banged. And it made him love her deeply for it.

The next day at work, Destiny again checked her personal email. There was a message from AFF. She checked the time and saw that the notification was received shortly after 10PM last night! She made a mental calculation and realized that wasn't very long after they had sent their reply. They were still awake but Destiny had shutdown her computer not expecting a reply so soon.

Destiny quickly looked around her. She sat in a cubicle and no one seemed to be standing around as she logged into AFF. She knew this was risky as people passing by her computer could see her monitor. She tried to keep the browser window as small as possible as she navigated to their inbox. There she found a message from 'black_knight215'. She checked again behind her and seeing that the coast was clear, opened the message.

"Dear Destiny,

I can appreciate that this is your first time meeting someone through AFF and I am happy to help guide you through it. First let me say that I was glad to hear that Mark was accepting of the conditions I laid out for us. I hope he wasn't too upset by my demands but I have found through some unfortunate experiences that it is best to set some ground rules and expectations before we get too far into this. As you may have noticed by now, I am the kind of person who knows what he likes and expects to get it that way. I hope this is not a problem for either of you. As for making phone contact before meeting in person, I never really saw the point in it. However, if it would make you feel more comfortable, I am willing to make an exception. I have never used the anonymous phone call feature within AFF so I don't know off-hand how it works. Personally, I would be fine with providing you with my cell phone number (see below) so you could call me at your convenience. I would prefer that you call me after 6:00PM though as I have a very busy schedule during the daytime and could not guarantee you I could talk for long.

Talk to you soon,

Ty
(215-555-6350)"

Destiny smiled to herself as she closed the browser window and thought, *how am I going to make it through the rest of the day?*

That evening, Mark had just walked through the door to find Destiny standing right there waiting to greet him. She was grinning provocatively as she proclaimed, "We got a response from Ty."

Mark could tell by the look on her face that Ty was still interested in meeting them.

Destiny led Mark to her computer where he found she had already logged into AFF and had Ty's message displayed. Destiny stood there quietly as Mark read the message. After Mark finished reading Ty's reply, he glanced down at the clock in the bottom corner of the desktop. It was just after six. Destiny said excitedly, "He actually replied last night shortly after we sent him a message. I didn't know about it 'til today when I got a notification from AFF."

Mark sat there and listened as he tried to absorb everything. He thought to himself, *things are moving really quickly now.*

Destiny asked, "Should we call him in a little bit?"

Mark hesitated responding to her question as he was feeling a little anxiety over actually talking to Ty directly. Finally, he overcame his anxiety and replied, "Yeah, let's do that…. In a little bit."

Mark then went to the bedroom to change into something more comfortable as he thought about their next steps. He came out to find Destiny in the kitchen washing dishes and asked, "So, what are we going to talk about when we call him?"

Destiny replied thoughtfully, "I've been thinking about that. I think we should just arrange for a time and place to meet."

Reminded of the MFM Guide they read, Mark thought Destiny was on the right track.

The article had said that getting to know your prospective third party personally before your first meeting could actually be a bad thing. After all, you're not looking to start a romance with this person; you just want to have sex. It helps to keep any romantic feelings in-check by minimizing unnecessary conversations.

Mark said, "I agree. Any ideas on when or where we should meet?"

Mark and Destiny had already discussed how they would like a first meeting to go. They had both agreed that meeting for a couple of drinks first and then heading to a hotel room would be a preferred approach. However, they had not picked any particular place for drinks or a hotel.

They discussed it for a while and finally decided on a hotel across town that catered mostly to people in town on business. The hotel had its own bar as well. They considered the possibility of running into someone they knew there and though it was a small chance but just in case, their plan was to say Ty was an old friend who lived elsewhere now and who had happened to be passing through town.

Now they just had to set a time, which would also depend on Ty's schedule. It was Tuesday and as much as they would like to meet Ty tonight, they both realized that Friday around seven would be a better time. This would allow them to have the rest of the weekend to recover from an entire night of wild sex and to deal with any emotional problems if they encountered any. Also, a few more days of abstinence would help to heighten their sexual tension and make the evening that much more enjoyable.

Destiny called the hotel just to make sure they had plenty of rooms available for Friday. They did.

Feeling they had pretty much covered their bases, Destiny asked, "Well, should we call him?"

Mark nodded and Destiny reached for her cell phone. She was about to dial when Mark said, "Wait!"

Destiny stopped as she looked up at him.

Mark said, "Aren't we supposed to call him anonymously?"

Destiny had visions of an encounter gone wrong and of a guy version of 'Fatal Attraction' who would not stop calling them.

Destiny replied, "Yeah, your right" as she put down her phone.

They were looking into the anonymous phone call service AFF provided for $20 a month when it occurred to Mark that he had a Skype account he rarely used. He felt that would provide an adequate level of protection from a phone stalker and suggested it to Destiny.

Mark logged into his old Skype account on Destiny's computer, and placed a call to his cell phone to verify that the microphone and speakers were working correctly. Then he hung-up and began to type in Ty's phone number. Before pressing the Dial button, he asked, "Who's going to do the talking?"

Destiny stared at him thoughtfully.

Mark said, "I think you should do most of the talking."

"Why me?" said Destiny with a nervous tone in her voice.

Mark replied, "Because you're who he wants to have sex with, not me" as he continued, "If I do all the talking, he may just change his mind about the whole thing. Besides, didn't he say he would prefer it if I didn't talk at all?" Mark smiled.

As Destiny thought about it she realized it made sense even though the MFM Guide suggested that the husband should handle all the communications. Destiny, nervous now, reluctantly agreed to do the talking. Mark pressed the dial button and as it rang Destiny asked, "What should I say?"

Before Mark could reply, they heard a deep voice answer, "Hello?" on the other end of the line.

Destiny said, "Hi...Ty? ...This is Destiny."

A moment of silence later Ty responded, "Oh, hi. How are you? I was wondering why my phone was showing a strange number. Are you using AFF to call me?"

Destiny answered, "No. Actually, we are using Skype to call you."

Ty said, "Oh. I see.... So Mark's there?"

Mark piped-in, "Hi, Ty."

Ty responded somewhat dryly, "Hi, Mark".

An awkward moment of silence passed before Ty said, "Well, I am looking forward to meeting you in person."

Almost simultaneously both Mark and Destiny proclaimed, "Yah," and Destiny finished with "...so are we" as she glared at Mark as if to say *'I thought I was going to do the talking?!'*

Ty asked, "So how do you want to do this? I'm actually kind of busy tonight but I should be available tomorrow. How about you?"

Destiny and Mark stared at each other for a second before Destiny responded, "Actually, we wondering if you would be available to meet Friday? ...If that works for you?"

A moment of silence passed before Ty said, "Friday...Hmmm. I think I could do that...What time?"

Destiny answered, "We were thinking around seven? ...If that works for you?"

Ty said, "Sure ... Where at?"

Destiny answered, "Well, we were thinking of the Marriott on the corner of 5th and Pine Street. It has a lounge where we could meet and have a few drinks first and then... maybe... move upstairs if you want."

Ty chuckled in a somewhat sinister yet sexy way and said, "Move upstairs. I like that," then more chuckles before continuing, "Seven sounds fine to me. We'll meet in the lounge and go from there."

Destiny asked, "You know where it is?"

Ty answered confidently, "Yeah , I know that place."

Another moment of silence passed and without anything more to say, Destiny tried to end the call with, "Well, we are really looking forward to meeting you."

Ty responded, "As am I" and surprisingly he continued with "So... this is your guy's first time, huh?"

Destiny, a little embarrassed now, answered apologetically, "Mmm, yeah. We are a little nervous. We have never done anything like this before."

Ty responded in a charming yet authoritative voice, "Well, don't be too nervous sugar. Daddy Ty is going to make sure you have a good time Friday night. Alright?"

Melting from the implication, Destiny managed to squeak, "Alright."

After a moment of silence Ty smoothly said, "So, I'll see you there. And until then, I'll be thinking about you."

Destiny squeaked again, "Alright" and added meekly "Bye."

Mark tried to add, "See you," but Ty had already hung up.

Sitting there, Destiny tried to regain her composure as she proclaimed, "Wow! He has a really sexy voice, huh?"

Mark acknowledged her with a nod. They were both surprised how easy the conversation went. They recognized that Ty had an ability to put people at ease. He also had the ability to turn-up the heat when he wanted to as he did at the end of the call. Destiny was still blushing from that.

Finally, Mark said, "So Friday."

Destiny replied, "Friday" and exhaled for a moment.

Mark asked, "So, should we reserve a room?"

Destiny coming back to her senses replied, "Oh yeah, I don't want to risk not being able to get one," as she turned back to the computer. She made reservations for Friday night and they went back to their usual evening activities as they tried not to think about how far away (and yet close) Friday was.

Each night, they slept restlessly as they counted down the days until Friday. They struggled to keep their commitment to abstinence and their dreams were filled with sex more than ever. They found it hard to concentrate at work and occasionally, they would speak about it, reassuring each other that this was something they both still wanted to do and they always seemed to agree that they did.

Chapter 5: Stepping Into A New World

At last, Friday came. They both struggled to function "normally" throughout the day. At midday, Destiny called Mark to see how he was doing. After talking it over, they both agreed to try and leave work a little early since neither of them could concentrate enough to get anything done.

Finally, at home getting ready for the evening, they at times found it hard to breathe with all the anticipation they were feeling, mixed-in with so many other emotions. It was already six and Destiny was still getting ready. She had been in the bathroom for over an hour and a half. Mark thought how much easier it was for a guy to dress-up. It had only taken him about thirty minutes (including the shower). He was wearing black trousers with a gray button-up long sleeve shirt - typical business casual attire.

Finally, Destiny came out of the bathroom. She was wearing another one of her tight black dresses. They considered having her wear the short tight dress she wore for the pictures, but they both decided it was a little too hot and would draw too much attention in the hotel lounge. This other dress was still sexy but only had a hint of sluttiness to it. It was something that some women could get away with wearing to work (depending on the job).

She finished off the ensemble with her black high-heel shoes, black stockings and a choke chain necklace. Destiny was stunning and sexy. Mark wanted her to wear her leather corset underneath but Destiny insisted that it showed through the dress too much, and besides, it became uncomfortable to wear after awhile. They had compromised and decided to stuff it in their overnight bag along with her pleather knee-high boots, a bottle of wine, wine glasses, candles and some other items. Their plan was for her to change into the lingerie once they brought Ty back to the room.

Mark looked over at the clock on the wall. It was now 6:10PM. Even though the Marriott was only about fifteen minutes away from them, they still had to check-in and get things set up in the room before meeting Ty in the lounge. Mark asked, "Ready?"

Destiny exhaled shakily as she replied, "Ready."

Mark grabbed the overnight bag and they headed towards the garage door.

They had discovered it was a lot easier to keep a handle on the tension and anxiety they felt when they were racing around trying to get to the hotel on time. Now, as they sat in the room, after going through the process of checking-in, the anxiety became overwhelming again. As Mark played with the clock radio beside the bed, searching for a radio station that played suitable music for the evening, Destiny noted the time on the radio and decided to compare it with the time shown on her cell phone, which she knew to be more accurate. They both said 6:46PM. Mark, satisfied with the station he selected, turned-off the radio and asked, "Should we go down?"

It was time, Destiny thought, as she replied, "Yeah, let's go."

They arrived in the lobby after taking the elevator down and headed over to the lounge. It was dark and there were not many people inside. A couple small groups of businessmen chatted at the high tables paying them no attention as they walked in. They quickly scanned the room looking for a table out of sight and away from others. They found a booth in the corner and tried to stealthily make their way towards it as they told themselves to just act natural and relax.

As they sat down across from each other, they scanned the room for a waitress, feeling they both could use a drink right about now. As they sat there making idle conversation, the situation felt surreal, as they both knew what was really on each other's mind right now.

The bartender made his way toward them and took their order. Shortly after, he returned with their drinks.

They made idle talk and occasionally Mark looked down at his watch, interrupting the conversation momentarily, and Destiny would ask, "What time is it?"

This time it was 7:05PM as Mark answered her.

Destiny, for her part, kept glancing over at the lounge entrance expectantly every time someone passed through the lobby.

They were almost done with their first order of drinks, which they had nearly guzzled, and began to look around for the bartender to order more when Destiny caught a dark figure rising up from a booth some ways down from them. With a drink in his hand, he began to make his way towards them and as he got closer, Destiny realized that it was Ty. As he arrived at the table smiling, he asked, "So, do you guys want to meet or not?"

Mark began to laugh although he didn't quite get the joke yet.

Destiny was suddenly aware that Ty had been sitting down from them all along.

She smiled as she asked, "You've been sitting there this whole time?"

Ty still smiling replied, "Yeah. You guys walked right past me when you walked in."

Mark said, "We did?" as Destiny apologized, "I'm sorry, we didn't see you. Why didn't you stop us as we walked by?"

Ty teasingly answered, "You guys looked like you could use a drink so I decided to let you get settled in first before I came over."

Ty was wearing a tight black shirt with short sleeves and no collar with gray slacks. He looked very chic and studly, Mark thought.

In the dim lighting, Destiny noticed his pectorals and a six-pack highlighted by his tight shirt. Ty was very tall, towering over them, with broad shoulders and huge biceps.

Destiny still smiling said, "Oh. You didn't have to wait for us to get settled," and motioned to him, "here, have a seat," as she slid over towards the center of the table.

Ty sat down across from Mark and next to Destiny. Still grinning he asked, "So, how are you two holding up so far?"

Both Destiny and Mark blushed a little as she confessed, "Still a little nervous but... doing OK otherwise."

Ty, replied, "Good, good," as he cast an appraising glance at Destiny.

A moment later his smile faded as he began to say in a more serious tone, "Well, unfortunately, I have some bad news. Something came up at work and I have to fly to Chicago tonight."

As that sunk in, Ty continued, "I would have called you but I don't have your phone number. Still, I didn't want to leave you guys thinking I stood you up. I do apologize."

Destiny, trying to hide her disappointment asked, "Well, how long can you stay?"

Ty replied, "I have to leave by eight-thirty at the latest."

Both Mark and Destiny tried to contain their disappointment. This was not something they had even considered could happen. They had been looking forward to tonight for days, really months. They understood that sometimes things come up and well, what can you do. But they were so close!

Mark asked, "How long are you gone for?"

Ty answered, "Until Tuesday."

After another moment of silence Ty said, "I know I promised you two a wonderful first time, but this is a trip I cannot get out of."

Mark said, "No, we understand completely. Don't worry about it."

Destiny had not said a word for awhile now. It was obvious that she was shattered.

Mark considered for a moment that maybe Ty had changed his mind about this at the last minute and was just making this up as a way to let us down easy. But, he didn't seem to be the kind of guy that would do that. Ty offered suggestively, "I do have until eight-thirty though," and let that sink in for a moment.

Destiny, starting to catch on to what Ty was hinting at thought, *it was just passed seven right now which would give us a little less than an hour and a half. Would that be enough time? Yes it would!*

Mark also caught on to what Ty was really trying to say which was that he didn't have much time. So if we wanted to do this, we shouldn't waste too much time talking.

Ty started to say, "Of course, if you want to try this some other time...."

Destiny interrupted him saying, "Oh no. We have already checked into a room. So if you want, we can finish our drinks quickly and..."

Ty interrupted as Mark was saying, "Yeah, we can..." and said, "Well, I don't want you guys to feel rushed or anything..."

Destiny, giggling now, tried to explain by saying, "I thought... We thought... you were saying that you couldn't... didn't have time for us tonight and that you just came here to tell us that before you had to leave."

Ty, understanding now, smiled and said, "Well, I would have like to spend more time with you on our first night together but... it is what it is."

Mark replied, "That's OK. We understand."

They were quiet for a moment and then Destiny asked with a tempting smile, "Well, should we go up to the room?"

Mark replied, "Let's" and began to stand up as the bartender arrived at the table and asked, "Can I get you guys another drink?"

Before Mark could answer, Ty answered for him, "No thanks, we are actually on our way out," and Ty began to stand up.

Mark was dimly aware that he had not paid for their drinks yet and fished out his wallet as he asked the bartender, "How much do we owe you?"

The bartender replied, "I can ring it up at the bar" and Mark followed him over there.

While Mark was waiting for the bartender to ring it up, he glanced back at their table and saw Ty sitting down again talking with Destiny. They both had large smiles on their faces as they conversed mischievously. He handed the bartender a twenty and waited for his change. Leaving a tip, Mark began walking back to their table. Destiny was snickering at something Ty had said as he arrived at the table. Ty turned to him and asked, "Ready?"

Mark nodded as Ty began to stand up again.

As they made their way to the elevator, Ty and Mark walked on opposite sides of Destiny. She said to Ty, "So, you'll be in Chicago until Tuesday you said?"

Ty responded, "Uh huh."

They stepped into the elevator and once the doors closed, she took in a deep breath and exhaled. Ty, grinning, as he looked her up and down asked, "Nervous?"

Destiny sighed a little and answered, "Just a little bit," while looking at the floor indicator above her.

They exited the elevator and without words, made their way down the empty hallway. Mark felt the hallway stretching out and fought the urge to walk faster as he was suddenly anxious to get them into the sanctuary of the room before someone could catch them in the hallway. Mark was sure that any person they encountered in the hallway would immediately know what the three were up to and he was beginning to feel conspicuous.

As they got closer to the room, Mark fished out the card key and walked ahead of them to have the door opened upon their arrival. As they stepped into the room, Mark closed the door behind them, reopened the door, and placed the 'Do Not Disturb' sign on the outside handle before closing it again.

Mark felt a wave of relief flood over him as they were now inside their own private sanctuary and free to engage in unspeakable sexual acts. And, he realized suddenly, he needed to use the bathroom.

As Mark turned towards the bathroom, he heard Destiny say to Ty, "Would you like some wine?"

Destiny was standing at the dresser preparing to open the bottle of wine as Ty, already making himself comfortable in one of the chairs, stood up, walked over to her and said charmingly, "Please. Allow me."

Destiny, a little stunned by how seductive he was, stood there looking into his eyes as Ty gently took the bottle of wine from her hands and began to open it. Finally, Destiny regained her composure and said, "Why thank you," with a smile.

Ty filled two glasses of wine and handed one to Destiny. Standing closely to Destiny, Ty clinked their glasses together and said softly, with the same level of charm, "Here's to new experiences."

Destiny, again struck by his deep, sexy voice, smiled softly while meeting his gaze and replied coyly, "To new experiences."

They both took a drink of wine to complete the toast. Then without warning, Ty leaned into Destiny, put his free arm around her back and they began to kiss each other softly.

Mark finished washing his hands in the sink, dried them and looked into the mirror at himself. He took a deep breath and thought to himself, "Well, here we go." He opened the door smoothly and walked out to find Destiny and Ty standing in front of the hotel dresser passionately kissing each other.

Adrenaline suddenly flooded his body and he became deeply aroused as he seemed to walk in slow motion into the room. Time seemed to stretch out as he watched Ty softly kissing his wife, her head slightly tilted back, with Ty's bent down and one hand supporting the small of her back. Mark thought, *wow. It's really happening.* Mark recalled all the nights they had spent talking about this first night and now that it had arrived, it felt surreal to Mark.

Mark tried to step quietly, trying not to disturb them and was disappointed when they, sensing his presence, broke off their kiss. They were still looking into each other's eyes as Mark searched for something to say to break this awkward silence he felt was caused by his intrusion into their private moment.

Mark slinked by them, next to the foot of the bed as he made his way to one of the chairs to sit down. Finally, Destiny regained her composure and took a step back from Ty. She reached out a hand to touch Ty's chest and said, "So. If you don't mind, I am going to change into something more comfortable."

Ty nodded and said smiling, "Take your time."

Destiny made her way to the bathroom to change. Mark, noting the word 'time', glanced at his watch. It was now 7:36PM and Mark thought 'time' wasn't something they had much of. Still, Ty didn't seem to be in any hurry.

As Ty returned to his seat, glass in hand, Mark stood up and made his way to the dresser to pour himself a glass of wine. As he did, Mark, trying to make conversation, asked, "So. What's in Chicago?"

Without missing a beat, Ty replied dismissively, "The Cubs."

Mark chuckled and thought to himself briefly, *maybe I was asking a question I had no right to ask*. But then Ty offered, "I have some business meetings to attend."

Mark replied simply, "Oh," as he walked over to turn on the radio.

Mark, not wanting to pry any further but not being able to stand the silence, ventured to ask Ty, "So, what do you do anyway?"

Ty took a drink from his glass and replied somewhat hesitantly, "I'm in the import/export business," and after a moment asked, "How about you?"

Before Mark could form a response, the bathroom door opened. Mark returned to his chair and was relieved at the interruption as it helped to put an end to this conversation, which seemed to be getting more awkward by the moment.

Destiny stepped out and turned to face them. Both Ty and Mark looked at her lustfully.

Mark was stunned to see Destiny wearing nothing but her leather corset, black stockings and her high-heel shoes. The corset was cupless, fully exposing her breasts and she wasn't even wearing any underwear. Her shaved pussy was completely exposed!

As she stood there, her body on full display, even Mark felt a little bit embarrassed and ashamed. Here was his wife, fully exposing herself to this stranger. In a depravity contrary to the moral standards of marriage, they were offering her body to this stranger, freely, as a sex toy to use for his own sexual gratification. It led Mark to wonder what kind of impression Ty had of them and especially of Mark for actually <u>encouraging</u> another man to have sex with his wife. On top of that, Mark couldn't help but to feel like he was a fool for agreeing to just sit on the sidelines and only watch while his wife and this stranger went at it. *I should have insisted on the option to join in if I wanted to.* Mark looked over to see Ty's reaction to all this.

Ty was grinning as he took in the view that Destiny was displaying solely for Ty's enjoyment. Mark could see from the look on Ty's face that passing judgment on her husband or their marital arrangement was the furthest thing from his mind right now. Finally, Ty said seductively, "Well, aren't you a bad little girl." Destiny blushed and began to giggle like a little schoolgirl in response.

Destiny was a little embarrassed by her childish outburst and fought to regain her self-control. Then she slowly began to walk towards them. As she walked, she slightly accentuated the movement of her hips from side to side and looked Ty straight in the eyes as she said in a seductive, teasing voice, "Well, maybe I just need to be punished. Anybody up for the task?" She over-acted the part standing before them now, her hands resting haughtily on her hips.

Mark was speechless as he listened to their exchange and thought how incredibly sexy Destiny looked and behaved. He had never seen her this way before. She seemed so naughty and completely in control of the situation as she played seduction games with Ty. Mark began to feel invisible in his chair as he suddenly felt very inadequate for Destiny. She was clearly capable of being so much more seductive and sophisticated with sexual flirtation than Mark could keep up with. Yet he felt extremely lucky to be married to such a beautiful, sexy, seductive wife, even if he was just now finding that out about her.

Ty, not intimidated at all by her seductive behavior, stood up and walked towards her with a slight swagger of his own until he stood almost up against her and in a velvety voice, replied slyly, "Well, that's exactly why Big Daddy is here now.... Isn't it?"

Destiny began blushing again. She realized she was out-matched and ouldn't come-up with a witty reply. Destiny dropped her hands to her side acknowledging her defeat. She realized that Ty was the one doing the real seducing here, not her. Destiny responded submissively, "I guess so."

Ty, still grinning, raised his hands to her waist as he looked deeply into her eyes. Ty went in for a kiss. Destiny's forearms and hands braced against his chest as he kissed her deeply. Ty's hands slid around her waist as he embraced her and found their way down over her bare behind.

Mark watched as Ty's massive hands cupped Destiny's behind and began to caress and gently squeeze her buttocks. He could hear Destiny moaning softly now as their mouths were joined together. Mark saw one of Destiny's hands sliding down Ty's chest; slowly down to his waistline as it probed for the growing bulge in his pants. Finding it, her hand rotated to grasp the outline of his long thick shaft and followed it as it snaked down his left pant leg.

Destiny slowly began to pull away from Ty's kiss. As she slowly looked downward to see this shaft her hand was grasping, she backed away slightly. Her eyes still fixed on this enormous cock shooting down his leg she began to slowly kneel before him. On her knees now, she began to meticulously undo the button and zipper.

Ty looked down at her as she worked.

Mark, sitting in his chair with quiet anticipation, began to rub the outline of his own cock as he continued to watch this scene unfold before him.

The radio beside the bed softly played a continuous set of slow dance music. Destiny could feel her heart beating with intensity as she slowly pulled Ty's pants and briefs down together as if one article of clothing. She felt them catch as she pulled slowly and decided pull with a little more firmness. As the clothing gave away, she was rewarded with the site of a massive shaft as it popped out and into view. With Ty's pants and briefs around his ankles, Destiny anxiously reached up for his long, thick, hot, black shaft.

Time seemed to slow to a crawl and the whole thing seemed dreamlike to Destiny as both her hands finally reached Ty's cock and wrapped around it. Destiny found she was able to wrap both hands around it end to end with length to spare. She couldn't recall ever being able to do that with any other men she had been with.

Destiny opened wide as she leaned forward, bringing Ty slowly into her mouth.

Ty responded by pulling his shirt off over his head. Putting it on the dresser, Ty reached down with his right hand and put it softly behind her head. Ty used his hand to help support and guide her as he gently pulled her deeper onto his cock.

Mark watched with exhilaration as Destiny brought Ty's manhood into her mouth. Mark's hand was still rubbing the outline of his pants and he began to work quietly to unbutton and unzip his own pants without disturbing the action taking place before him.

Destiny found it hard to get much of Ty inside of her mouth before she began to have a gag reflex. She was disappointed with herself and was resolved to do something about it later. Mark had shown her an amateur video of a wife giving oral pleasure to a black man. This woman, much to both Mark and Destiny's surprise, seemed to have a talent for swallowing her stud's rather large cock all the way to the base. Destiny suspected she had spent a lot of time practicing with smaller inanimate objects before attempting it on a real cock. Destiny now made a mental note to herself that later she would practice taking her dildos deep into her mouth so she could do this for her black stud, too.

Ty enjoyed Destiny's repeated efforts to swallow him deeply but was anxious to put it between her legs. He bent over to lift Destiny up by the shoulders.

Destiny released Ty's cock from her mouth and struggled to catch her breath as she began to stand up following Ty's lead. Standing there, waiting for guidance, Ty delicately turned her to the side and gently motioned her to sit on the end of the bed as Ty began to remove the rest of his clothes.

Mark watched Destiny sitting on the edge of the bed trying to catch her breath. Her eyes where watery and her face was red and attentive as she watched Ty removing his clothes. The look on her face showed that she was very eager to continue.

Wiping tears from her eyes, which were caused by her attempts to swallow Ty, Destiny took the brief respite in activities to glance over at Mark to see how he was taking it.

Mark saw her brief look that said 'Wow!' and then changed to 'how are you doing? Are you OK?' but before he could show his own reaction, she impatiently turned back to Ty who was still removing his clothing and shoes.

Mark could see that Destiny was becoming impatient. He could see she was already getting worked up into a sexual frenzy and she was even absent-mindedly massaging her own clit as she eagerly watched and waited for Ty to finish and return his attentions to her. Mark knew then that Destiny would not deny any of Ty's desires tonight.

Ty was very meticulous with his clothes. He removed his shoes and socks and put them on the floor directly below the TV. The he removed his pants and underwear, folding them patiently, before placing them neatly next to the TV set. Destiny, still breathless, watched as he finally folded his shirt and put it on top of the stack of clothes.

Ty then turned to Destiny who was still sitting on the foot of the bed.

Mark watched as she looked up at Ty, her eyes wide and filled with anticipation; she awaited his instructions.

Ty reached down to her, spread her legs and lifted them up causing Destiny to roll onto her back.

Destiny, a little startled, looked up at him and wondered what was coming next.

Mark looked on as Ty, still holding Destiny legs up by her thighs and in one continuous motion, began slowly pushing Destiny up towards the pillows as he climbed onto the bed behind her. He effortlessly continued to slide her body smoothly across the sheets until her head was nearly up against the headboard.

Shocked and impressed at Ty's show of strength and finesse, Destiny quickly shot a glance over to Mark that said 'Oh my god! Did you see that?'

Mark, too, was impressed. He couldn't believe how effortlessly and delicately Ty was able to manhandle Destiny into position.

Without words, Ty edged up between Destiny's spread legs with his huge, stiff cock aiming directly at Destiny's pussy. As the distance closed, Mark envisioned for a moment, it was like watching a missile as it honed in on its target.

Ty lowered himself onto Destiny and the two began kissing.

After a couple of minutes of watching them kiss, Mark suddenly felt too visible and exposed; he decided it was too bright in the room. He remembered that Destiny had brought candles and she had placed them around the room shortly after they arrived. Mark got up, and while holding his pants up with one hand, went around the room lighting the candles. He then went over to the dresser and turned off the light. With the room illuminated solely by candlepower now, Mark returned to his chair. Ty and Destiny said nothing about the change in lighting and seemed oblivious to everything around them as they continued to kiss.

Destiny kept her legs spread wide, inviting Ty into her body as they softly kissed.

Eventually, Ty pulled slowly up and away from her. She looked expectantly into his eyes as he now hovered over her with a subtle smile forming across his face. The smile seemed to say to her 'Are you ready for this?'

She knew what was coming next would be incredible. Destiny stared wide-eyed and expectantly into Ty's face as he slowly reached for his cock with one hand and began to guide it into her wetness.

Destiny's body shuddered as the head entered her. She immediately recognized that it felt nothing like the cold, non-pliable shape of the dildos she had been using. No, this felt much better... Ty's cock, throbbing, felt warm and alive. As Ty continued to guide it in her, Destiny felt a surge of warmth flooding through her body. She felt all her tension and anticipation begin to wash away and as she closed her eyes, she began to sense a strange feeling that she hadn't experienced in a long time. Destiny was ready to surrender herself to Ty.

Mark slowly stroked his now fully erect penis. He had to fight the urge to stroke it harder and faster, as he knew the night was still young. Sometimes, he had to stop stroking it altogether, or else he would lose control. No, he wanted to hold himself there as long as possible, just on the edge of ejaculation. Mark looked on as Ty, ever so slowly, inserted himself deeper into his wife. Mark's entire body shuddered at that thought, *His WIFE! His wife was getting fucked by this incredible stud and all he could do was just sit there, with his tiny penis in his hand and watch. This was really happening.* The thought suddenly made his body shudder more violently this time and he caught himself letting out an audible whimper. He fought to get control of himself as he hoped they hadn't heard his uncontrolled outburst.

The room was quiet and Ty was about half way in Destiny when suddenly, she let out a loud moan.

Mark was startled out of his thoughts and he momentarily wondered if anybody was in the two adjacent rooms. *Surely they would have heard that sound,* he thought to himself.

Ty, chuckling now, asked Destiny, "Feel good?"

She replied less loudly this time with, "Oh my god! Yes!"

It occurred to Mark that Destiny had just had her first orgasm of the night.

As the room grew quiet again, Mark began to notice Destiny emitting new sounds. At first they were barely audible, as if she was experiencing hypothermia and taking short quick gasps of air. But as the noises grew in volume, they began to carry with them a desperate whimper.

Ty was almost all the way inside her now and hearing the sounds she was making, Ty stopped and asked in a soft, concerned voice, "Are you OK?"

After a moment, her sounds began to subside and finally she answered reassuringly, with a whimper still in her voice, "I'm OK. It's just... really deep."

Ty, visibly disappointed, sensed the discomfort he was causing her and retracted himself from her by a couple of inches.

Destiny gasped, and then began to plead, "It's OK. Don't stop, I can handle it."

As she pleaded it was clear to Mark that she absolutely did not want to disappoint Ty. Destiny didn't want Ty to think she couldn't handle his manhood.

Ty considered for a moment the contradiction between her words and the look of pain on her face. He could also see a growing desperation in her face that suggested she didn't want him to stop, that she wanted to feel pain from this. Then with understanding, Ty began to smile into her concerned face. Finally he said grinning, "I know you can."

As Destiny looked up into his face in fear of what was to come if he knew what she truly wanted, Ty abruptly shoved himself deep back inside her again. Destiny nearly screamed, caught herself, and then panted reassuringly, "I'm OK. Don't stop." Much to Destiny's relief, Ty didn't stop. Instead he just wickedly smiled back at her as he began a slow, deep, rhythmic, pumping motion. Destiny realized then that he had no intention of stopping or even holding back. She thought to herself, *oh my god. This is it. This is what I remember being 'taken' by a man feels like.*

Until now, Destiny wasn't sure if she would or even could experience that feeling again from so long ago. But here she was and it was exactly the way she remembered it.

Eventually, Ty's face turned up and away from her as he began to pump her more fervently. Ty become lost in his own passion.

At first, Mark could see Destiny was visibly holding back the pain she felt. Unable to hold it in anymore, she turned her face to the side and began to let controlled gasps and even grunts escape with every stroke Ty made.

Ty continued to ignore her as Mark could see wrinkles forming on her forehead; her eyes tightly closed and teeth clenching. Mark thought he should say something but he was extremely turned on as he watched Ty fucking her mercilessly. Mark stroked himself hard and then felt cum oozing down his cock.

Ty paused for a moment to put her legs up between his arms as he grabbed a firm hold of Destiny by her hips and began slamming his cock deep inside her as hard as he could.

Destiny began to scream uncontrollably.

Mark could see Destiny was in serious pain now and he reflexively jumped up to save her.

Destiny stopped screaming just as Mark stood up and she gave Mark a look that stopped him in his tracks. She was shaking her head in a way that suggested she didn't want him to intervene.

Mark was confused and wasn't sure what he should do as Destiny motioned with her eyes for Mark to sit back down. He could see the pain on her face but she was clearly telling him not to try and stop Ty.

Mark sat back down in his chair and began absently stroking his cum soaked cock. He was dimly aware that someone could be knocking on their door any second now to find out what was going on in here.

Ty continued to fuck Destiny as hard as he could and still, Destiny refused to give in and call for mercy.

Mark was again beginning to feel compelled to stand up and intervene, to stop this madness before Destiny got seriously hurt. Selfishly, he didn't want to, but for Destiny's sake he felt he had to. But Mark was unsure how. He was unsure if he could stop Ty at this point even if he wanted to. Ty was much stronger than he was and Mark tried to imagine himself trying to wrestle Ty off of his wife.

Mark noticed he was getting hard again as he thought, *Destiny is getting the shit fucked out of her and I can't do anything to stop it.*

He then began to notice something new in Destiny's voice that gave him pause. The sounds she was making, her grunting, her breathing; now becoming more steady and rhythmic. It somehow sounded like a pain <u>and</u> pleasure sound to Mark. He also noticed the resigned look on her face. This was something new, something he hadn't seen in her before. Destiny seemed to be defying the pain as if she intended to conquer it somehow; to somehow turn it into something else - to turn it into… pleasure!

All at once it came to Mark. Like a ton of bricks he realized that this is what Destiny meant by being 'taken'. Destiny had tried to explain to Mark how she felt when she was being 'taken' and now Mark could see it with his very own eyes.

Mark's heart dropped and adrenaline flowed through his body as he watched Ty fucking Destiny as hard as he could. Mark began stroking himself hard and fast, uncontrollably, aware that he was now moaning loudly himself but he didn't care anymore as he saw the look on Destiny's face, a mix of pain and pleasure, a look he had never seen before, he exploded violently all over himself, moaning loudly as he did.

Destiny hadn't even noticed Mark's orgasm, for she had been lost in her own series of orgasms for several minutes now. It started shortly after Ty began fucking her as hard as he could and hadn't stopped since. After each orgasm subsided, she began to feel extreme pain and was sure she couldn't take it anymore. Then, suddenly, she would be overtaken by another orgasm and then another. She lost count of the individual orgasms as they sometimes seemed to merge together.

After several more minutes went by, what seemed to be an eternity to Destiny, she felt Ty turn rock hard inside her pussy. Then Ty began to roar something primal as he exploded inside her.

His thrusting motions slowly began to fade away, eventually stopping altogether. He gently collapsed onto her and she wrapped her arms around him and held him there in a soft embrace.

Ty was breathing heavily as he lie on her trying to catch his breath, droplets of sweat forming over his body.

Destiny, too, was breathing heavily and sweating. Her pussy throbbed with immense pain but it was a very satisfying feeling. She felt completely fulfilled and the pain she still felt was somehow very gratifying.

Mark was lost in a state of bliss. He was still slowly, uncontrollably, stroking his now limp cum laden penis. His upper body was rhythmically rocking back and forth in his chair. His eyes were narrow as he stared blankly over into the direction of Ty and Destiny.

As Destiny came back to present reality she became aware of a creaking chair sound coming from the corner of the room. With Ty's full weight pressing down on her holding her immobilized, she could only manage to tilt her head to the side and down to see what was making the sound. She saw Mark there in some kind of trance as he rocked back and forth in his chair stroking his limp penis and staring blankly back at her.

Mark was then suddenly aware that Destiny was looking at him. He quickly tried to regain his composure as he stopped rocking and tried to sit more upright in his chair. He took a deep breath and let it out loudly in a way of saying to Destiny, 'Wow!'

Destiny stared back at Mark. She was still breathing heavily and her face was glistening with sweat. A smile began to spread across her face as she realized just how much Mark had enjoyed watching her being taken. Destiny was immensely relieved as she had been afraid that Mark might not be able to handle seeing her being taken by a man in the way that she wanted to be.

She looked at Mark and asked with her eyes "You liked that? Good. So did I."

They continued to gaze at each other for a brief while longer - lovingly, knowingly.

Eventually, Ty began to stir and Destiny tilted her head back towards Ty as he began to climb off of her. He stopped half way up and came back down to give Destiny a kiss. Pulling away again, he tried to catch his breath as he looked down into Destiny's face and said, "Thanks. I really needed that."

Destiny smiled back and replied, "No. Thank You," before adding, "I really needed that," as she giggled.

Ty responded, "I guess you did."

Destiny began to blush.

Ty climbed off the bed and glanced over at the alarm clock and asked, "Is that time right?"

Destiny looked over at the clock and answered with some concern, "Yes, it is."

Ty said, "I gotta get going," as he headed towards the bathroom.

It was eight-thirty on the dot. As the bathroom door closed behind Ty, Destiny moved to sit upright in the bed. She pulled the sheets up over her legs as she leaned back against the headrest.

Mark began to clean himself off. There was a washcloth on the table beside him and he used it.

Destiny, still trying to catch her breath a little bit, watched Mark as he cleaned himself up. Finished, he buttoned and zipped up his trousers.

Mark looked over at Destiny, noticing that she had been watching him clean up. Destiny was smiling and seemed very satisfied. Mark smiled back and asked, "You have fun?"

Destiny nodded up and down enthusiastically before asking, "How about you?"

Mark answered with conviction, "Absolutely."

Before they could say more, the door to the bathroom opened and Ty walked out. Ty walked over to his clothes to get dressed. As they watched Ty getting dressed, he said smiling, "Well, I hate to eat and run...."

Mark responded, "Oh no, of course...."

Destiny finished for Mark, "...you got a plane to catch," and then she said cautiously, "I hope we can meet again."

Ty, still getting dressed, responded without looking at them, "How about next Friday?"

Destiny and Mark shot a look at each other, they both smiled and Destiny turned back to look at Ty and said in a cheerful, enthusiastic voice, "Sounds great!"

Finished getting dressed, Ty looked over to Destiny and said, "Great. Just give me a call sometime next week and we will work out the details."

Destiny nodded as she said, "OK." With nothing more to say, Ty smiled as he began to slowly walk over to Destiny.

Mark watched as Destiny got up onto her knees, throwing the covers off of her in the process. She moved over to the edge of the bed and as she kneeled there, she reached out her arms just as Ty arrived beside the bed.

Ty bent over slightly and kissed her as his arms went around her shoulders and her hands rested on his hips. Ty began to pull away for a moment then changed his mind as he went in for another kiss. This time he pulled her in close and embraced her tightly. Mark watched as they began to kiss more deeply.

Destiny was still wearing her corset and black stockings as she kneeled there at the edge of the bed. They held each other tightly while they kissed.

Ty pulled away again and said smiling, "I gotta go."

Destiny replied smiling, "Uh huh." And Ty went in for another kiss. Mark watched as Ty's black hands slid slowly down her back and over her hourglass shaped waist to rest on her bare white ass. Mark couldn't help but to see just how beautiful they looked together. Mark realized that watching them have sex that night was the most erotic and sexually fulfilling experience he had ever had. He also now realized that although he loved Destiny very much, their relationship had been missing something all this time.

Mark now knew that Destiny could never reach her full sexual potential with just Mark as her lover. Mark knew that Destiny needed a special kind of man like Ty that could dominate her in the bedroom in a way that Mark never would be able to. Mark envied Ty for his physique and large package but knew he couldn't do much about that. Instead, Mark thought about how he had also been missing out on a kind of sexual fulfillment that he never even thought was possible. Now that Mark had a taste of what he had been missing all his life, Mark knew that bringing a man like Ty into their bedroom to service Destiny on an occasional basis would allow both of them to experience a much higher level of sexual fulfillment in their relationship.

Ty and Destiny continued to kiss as Destiny began to moan softly with pleasure.

Mark began to wonder if this was going to go on for much longer as he was already getting another erection and desperately wanted to stroke himself into another eruption as he watched these two making love before him. Unfortunately, only a few more seconds passed before Ty, again, began to release her from his embrace.

As he pulled away, Mark saw Destiny not wanting to let go; not wanting the kiss to end yet, she leaned forward to kiss him again until she was about to fall off the bed. Finally, she reluctantly let go and sat back on her knees as they smiled into each other's faces.

Ty walked backwards for a moment smiling at Destiny's adoring face before he turned towards the door.

As the door closed behind Ty, Destiny continued to sit there on her knees as she faced the door longingly. Moments past and it suddenly occurred to Mark that Destiny looked much like a lost puppy longingly and patiently waiting for her master to return. At that moment, Mark saw that Destiny, sitting there in her black leather corset staring at the door, was the most beautiful, sexiest woman in the world.

Mark's heart pounded again, he felt his penis come fully erect, as he realized he wanted to make love to her like never before. Mark stood up and began to frantically remove his pants. Destiny turned to see what all the commotion was about. She smiled and asked, "So what do you think?"

Mark replied impatiently, "About what?" as he was trying to remove his shoes.

"About Ty, silly." she said.

Mark answered, "I think he's great."

Destiny replied, "So do I," as Mark jumped into bed.

Her eyes widened as she tried to figure out what Mark was up to exactly. Mark grabbed her by the shoulders and threw her back down on the bed. Startled, Destiny said smiling, "Easy there, big boy." Mark forcefully spread her legs and thrust his face into her wet pussy. Mark's tongue searched deep into Destiny's pussy as he licked up her juices.

Mark was frantically grinding his groin into the bed sheets as he ate her. Destiny had never seen Mark this worked up before and as she grappled with Mark's suddenly raging sex drive, Destiny saw Mark move up to insert his fully erect penis into her.

Mark plowed into Destiny's sopping wet pussy with his penis. It slid in very easily.

As Mark lay on Destiny, she put her arms around him smiling with understanding, as he jerked manically inside her. Mark was already breathing heavily as he pumped Destiny with short, quick strokes. Destiny laid there calmly with a smile spreading across her face, as she held Mark tightly to her. Breathing heavily into her ear, Mark pumped away in hard, fast and short strokes. After a couple of minutes, Destiny felt Mark's whole body go rigid for a moment as he released inside her.

Mark jerked as he continued to thrust his pelvis into Destiny for almost another minute before his thrust began to weaken and he could thrust no more.

Destiny held him in her embrace, as he breathed deeply in her ear. As his breathing slowed, Destiny, her pussy still numb from Ty's pounding, dimly wished she could have felt more of Mark's penis inside of her. No matter, she thought, she loved Mark dearly and was content with the fact that she had had enough orgasms for one night, anyway.

Her thoughts turned uncontrollably to Ty, and the incredible orgasms she had as she was 'taken' in the way she remembered so many years ago. Then, for a moment, she caught herself imagining it was Ty's body laying on her right now instead of Mark's. Her body quivered momentarily at the thought before she put it away.

Thoroughly satisfied with the evening, she became dimly aware that Mark had actually fallen asleep on top of her. She smiled, and held him there as she tried to remember if Mark had ever fallen asleep on her before. She couldn't remember. Slowly, she slipped into unconsciousness herself.

Half an hour later, Mark stirred and awoke to find himself laying on Destiny. He gently rolled off of her, trying not to wake her and lay by her side. She rolled over onto her side and the two fell back to sleep.

They slept deeply and without dreams that night.

Once, Destiny, feeling uncomfortable, awoke and realized she had to go to the bathroom. Finished, she stood up and looked into the mirror for awhile. Then, she removed her corset, laid it on the counter and returned to bed as she thought fondly about their extraordinary evening. It felt like a dream now, like it didn't really happen.

Lying back down, she smiled at the subtle pain she felt in her groin, an indication that it really did happen. Smiling, she fell back to sleep.

The next morning, Mark stirred and awoke.

As he tried to take in his surroundings, the previous night came flooding back into his memories. He began to replay the events in his head as he thought to himself, *Wow... We actually did it... And it was great! Even better than I imagined it would be.*

Mark was pleased with their conquest. He thought about how sexy Destiny had been through it all, and how he discovered the sounds she had made and the look on her face when he saw her being 'taken' for the first time. Mark could feel his penis becoming erect at the thought.

Destiny stirred and Mark rolled over to find her lying on her side facing away from him. Mark slid closer to Destiny spooning her from behind as his now hard penis pushed in between her legs. He laid an arm gently over her shoulder to rest his hand on her breast.

Destiny dimly became aware of Mark massaging one of her nipples. She opened her eyes to see she was in a hotel room and then began to remember why she was there as a smile formed across her face.

Mark, aware that Destiny was awake now, began to guide his penis up into her already wet hole. Destiny lifted her leg obligingly as Mark proceeded to make soft thrusting motions. Mark began kissing her neck. Mark's penis fell out as he was unable to make full penetration from this angle. Mark tried to guide his wet penis inside her again and found that he had put it against the wrong hole.

Destiny softly said, "Go ahead."

Mark paused for a moment trying to understand what she meant by that. He finally understood and he began to slowly push it in. As it suddenly entered, Destiny let out a soft moan. Mark pulled Destiny closer by her hips causing it to slide all the way in.

Mark felt blissful as he slowly, gently thrust himself in and out of her.

Destiny couldn't help herself as she began to recollect the previous evening's activities while Mark was softly thrusting her from behind. She closed her eyes and thought about Ty having his way with her...again.

After awhile, they climaxed together. They lay there for a short while longer as Mark held her closely.

Eventually, Mark lifted his head and kissed Destiny on the cheek and whispered softly into her ear, "I love you babe."

Destiny turned her head toward him smiling and replied with sincerity, "I love you, too."

Smiling into each other's faces, Mark began to move back from her and get out of bed.

Destiny smiled at Mark and thought about how much she really did love him as he made his way to the bathroom. Destiny heard the shower turn on as she rolled on to her back.

Destiny thought how lucky she was to be married to Mark. She wondered how many other men out there would be willing to allow their wives to explore their sexuality with another man. As she considered this, laying on her back in bed, she became aware that her fingers were unconsciously massaging her clit. She fantasized about her next encounter with Ty until she climaxed.

Mark finished his shower and upon exiting the bathroom, found Destiny standing at the dresser making coffee. She said doubtfully, "I don't know how good this is going to be," as she handed Mark a cup.

Mark took the cup, leaned into Destiny and gave her a kiss. She smiled at him as she made her way to the bathroom.

After taking a shower, Destiny exited the bathroom to find Mark packing their overnight bag. *Good,* she thought to herself. Destiny had been thinking in the shower about how she wanted to get back home and was glad to see Mark working towards that end.

In the car, as they drove the short distance home, their thoughts were about the prior evening. They were quiet for the most part. Twice they turned to look at each other and then smiling, they broke into laughter. They enjoyed the fact that they had shared a very special experience together now, an experience that neither of them could ever consider telling to somebody else, a secret they would carry to the grave, and this bond made them feel closer than ever before.

Arriving home, they went in and unpacked their overnight bag. Finished, they went about their usual weekend rituals independently as things returned to normal. Occasionally, as they were passing by each other, they would knowingly smile to each other, or embrace and have a short kiss before continuing on with their tasks.

That night, as they went to bed, they found they had no desire to have sex. They were still content with the previous night's experience and felt no sexual tension that had to be released. Destiny made a mental note to herself, "Tomorrow, I need to start deep throat training," before eventually falling asleep.

By Tuesday evening, life had returned to its normal routine except that Mark and Destiny somehow felt much closer to each other than they had ever felt before. Destiny noticed that Mark spent a lot more time kissing and holding her. From Mark's point of view, he saw Destiny as a very different woman now. She seemed to be much more feminine to him than he had realized before. Mark supposed she had always been this feminine but that he just had a hard time seeing it until he saw her coupled with Ty.

Now when Mark looked at her, he was often reminded of her and Ty in the throes of passion and how beautiful they looked together. This filled Mark's heart with affection and admiration for Destiny and he found himself kissing and touching her more often and with more passion than ever before.

Chapter 6: Exploring Their New World

They had just returned home from their respective jobs. Destiny had started a load of laundry when she remembered that Ty was returning from Chicago today and that she intended to call him tonight after work to arrange their next meeting.

Destiny often found herself recollecting the events of last Friday night and was already anxiously anticipating their next get together even though in the days since then, her affections for Mark had seemed to grow stronger than ever.

She briefly considered the fact that another interlude with Ty could actually put this strong bond she now felt with Mark in jeopardy. However, she realized that it was in fact this very experience with Ty that had strengthened her and Mark's relationship to begin with. She wondered if that one night with Ty should be enough for her and she recognized it wasn't. Destiny decided she wanted more and she knew that Mark wanted more, too.

Destiny went to the family room were Mark was watching the news and said, "We're supposed to call Ty tonight."

Mark turned to Destiny and thought about what she was saying. Finally, he replied, "Oh yeah, I almost forgot."

Mark glanced at the clock on the wall and continued, "It's 6:30. Do you want to call him now?"

Destiny wondered if Mark was actually satisfied for now but didn't want to say no to her. Should she push the issue? They had not even discussed the issue of their next meeting with Ty until now. Destiny was pretty sure that Mark still wanted her to bed Ty again this Friday but thought she better make absolutely sure.

As she tried to read Mark's face, she asked in a concerned voice, "Do you still want to get together Friday?"

Mark replied reassuringly, "Yeah. I would like that. Do you?"

A seductive smile formed across Destiny's face as she answered, "Well, I've been thinking about it... A lot."

Mark was suddenly aroused by the notion that Destiny was craving some playtime with her stud. Mark rose from the couch and said with finality, "Then let's call him."

They went to Destiny's office and she began to log into Mark's Skype account. Ready, she turned to Mark who was just sitting down and asked, "Where do we want to meet? Same place, same time?"

Mark answered, "That's fine."

It occurred to Mark that it cost $130 last time to stay at the Marriot. He began to add, "Well... yeah. That's fine."

Sensing Mark's hesitation, Destiny asked, "What?"

Mark explained, "Nothing. I was just thinking it cost over $130 last time but... don't worry about it."

Destiny asked in a concerned voice, "You sure?"

Mark realized that last Friday night he had the most intense and satisfying sexual experience ever and that it was foolish to quibble over money when he had the opportunity to experience such pleasure again. Mark knew he was hooked. He would do just about anything and pay virtually any amount just to see Destiny coupled with Ty again. Mark said with conviction this time, "Yeah. That's fine."

Destiny, reassured, turned to her computer to call.

After two rings, Ty answered and said, in a deep charming voice, "Hello, Destiny."

Destiny, caught off guard, instantly felt herself melting at his voice. She gathered herself and replied, trying to imitate his inflection, "Hello, Ty," and then added curiously, "How did you know it was us?"

Ty answered, "I recognized the strange number."

As Destiny momentarily found herself at a loss for words, Ty continued, "So how are you guys doing?"

Destiny, smiling now, answered, "We're doing fine," and then added, "How was your trip?"

Ty answered with disinterest, "It was OK."

Destiny searched for something to say and asked, "So, what are you up to?"

Ty answered casually, "Getting ready to go out with some friends."

Destiny, in a concerned voice, asked, "Oh, I hope we are not keeping you?"

Ty answered simply, "You're not," and then after a moment of silence continued with interest, "So do you guys still want to meet Friday?"

Destiny, feeling a little uncomfortable with the small talk, was relieved to get to the point and answered, "Yes...in fact that's why we're calling...to see if you are still available...same time, same place?"

After a moment of silence, Ty responded unsurely, "Hmm... the Marriott...."

Destiny, sensing hesitation in his voice interjected, "Or we could try someplace else if you want?"

Ty responded, still somewhat hesitantly, "No... that's fine. Do you want me to pick up the bill this time?"

Destiny, caught off guard by his proposal, thought about it quickly and realized that she preferred they had control of the room and... he still seemed hesitant about the Marriott. Finally, she offered, "No. That's fine. We...Well...What about our place instead?"

Mark shot a surprised look at Destiny but she ignored it as she awaited Ty's response.

Mark thought about it and remembered the uncomfortable feeling he had in the lounge, the lobby and the hallway. As if people were looking at them, aware of what they were up to. Mark actually preferred the idea of meeting Ty in the comfort of their own home but the articles he read strongly recommended against it (at least for the first meeting) just in case the person turns out to be unstable.

But Mark had met Ty and he didn't seem unstable at all and he figured they would need to invite him over eventually as Mark was sure he didn't want this to be the last time Ty and Destiny got together. In fact, although he hadn't shared these intentions with Destiny, Mark was already hoping that both Ty and Destiny would eventually establish a long-term sexual affair together.

Although Mark didn't want to risk losing Destiny to Ty and he didn't want Destiny to think he didn't cherish her as much as he actually did, he also realized that he desperately wanted to see Destiny getting ravished on a regular basis and in such a way that only someone like Ty could accomplish. At least if Mark was going to continue to feel as gratified as he did last Friday, he needed this arrangement to work somehow. Mark was sure Destiny wouldn't protest too much at being ravished by Ty on regular basis either.

Mark prayed that bringing Ty into their bedroom wouldn't, over time, lead to an end to his and Destiny's relationship and he even hoped that, with Ty's help, this would actually bring them closer together just as it had done over the past few days. Finally, Mark shrugged his shoulders resigning himself to Destiny's proposal to invite Ty to their home.

Ty replied, "If you guys are comfortable with that," and then added sarcastically, "You know, it's not like I'm going to stalk you or anything," and laughed.

Destiny suddenly realized that she had in a way insulted him. Why was she being so guarded with a man she had just shared herself with so intimately just a few days ago? She could see how that could be a little bit insulting to him; as if they still didn't trust him after everything they had already been through together.

Destiny said apologetically, "You're right. I'm sorry. Of course we would like to invite you to our home."

Ty, still chuckling asked teasingly, "Are you sure?"

Destiny, offered again, sincerely as she tried to explain, "I'm sorry. I didn't think..." and then, wanting to move on from her embarrassment, added in a more cheerful tone, "Do you got a pen?"

Ty's laughing faded as he confirmed, "I do."

Destiny proceeded to give Ty their street address then Ty asked, "How's 8:30 sound?"

Destiny glanced at Mark seeking consensus and turned back to the computer and answered, "8:30 is fine," and then decided to add teasingly, "You don't have a plane to catch this time, do you?"

Ty laughed as he answered, "No. At least none that I am aware of."

After a moment, Ty said optimistically, "So. I will see guys at 8:30 Friday night then," as if to end the conversation but then quickly added, "And if something does come up, what number can I reach you at?"

Destiny considered it. *Well. He has our home address now so why not our phone number too?* And then answered, "Actually...why don't you call us at this number....Ready?"

Ty acknowledged, "Uh huh."

Destiny proceeded to give Ty their home number.

Mark didn't protest.

Ty said, "OK. 8:30 then."

Destiny said in a soft voice, "Bye," and Ty hung up.

Mark and Destiny sat there thoughtfully for a moment and then Mark said jokingly, "Well. No sex 'til Friday."

Destiny laughed.

Friday evening Destiny was in the bathroom getting ready for their encounter with Ty. Mark came in to check on her. He informed her, "It's 8:10."

Destiny responded slightly irritated at being rushed, "I know. I'm almost done."

Having performed his duty, Mark made his way to the living room. He decided to put some music on and selected a compilation CD of slow dance songs. He then lit some candles and dimmed the lights.

Mark thought how much more comfortable he felt this night compared to last Friday when he had difficulty concentrating on the simplest tasks as his thoughts were consumed with the anticipation of their first meeting. This time, however, for most of the week he had not even thought much about this approaching day. It seemed Destiny was much more relaxed too. He thought, *we haven't even had our second date with Ty and already it feels like it's just become another part of our relationship. Just an alternate lifestyle we engage in and keep hidden from our friends and family.* Mark found this thought warmly arousing. That's when Mark began to feel a growing anticipation for this night and the nights to come. He tried to put those feelings away for now thinking to himself, *it isn't time yet. Later.*

Having set the mood, he went to the wine rack in the kitchen and selected a bottle he knew Destiny would like. Mark wasn't much of a wine drinker himself so Mark went to the refrigerator and selected a bottle of beer instead. He opened it and took a swig. He thought about Ty. *What does he drink?* He thought back to their time in the lounge. Ty had carried a glass over to the table and Mark could recollect it looked like Coca-Cola, ice and possibly some-liquor. Mark knew they had Coke in the fridge, ice and a fully stocked bar in the corner. He was sure he had whatever it was that Ty would like to drink.

Mark decided to open the bottle of wine for Destiny. He poured a glass and brought it to Destiny to help take the edge off the evening. Destiny was still in the bathroom getting ready.

Handing the glass to her, she gave him a genuine smile and said, "Thank you honey."

Mark could see Destiny had chosen to wear the slutty black dress tonight. The one she wore when he took her picture. Also, he noticed that she had put her leather corset on, this time under her dress. She was also wearing her over-the-knee pleather boots this time. Something he remembered she hadn't put on back in the hotel bathroom when she changed into her corset.

Mark remembered how he had felt when he saw her walk out of the bathroom that night, as she exposed herself to Ty for the first time. Mark felt his heart begin to pump faster as he thought about the sexy show she put on for Ty as she walked towards him. He tried to put it out of his mind. *Not yet,* he thought to himself. Mark left Destiny to finish getting ready for Ty and made his way to the living room again.

He sat there trying to think more normal thoughts, of something not as arousing as he waited for the doorbell to ring. It occurred to him that the abstinence they had observed all week was beginning to affect him profoundly now as he felt a growing anticipation and excitement flow through his body. He was beginning to feel the same way he felt last Friday. Mark began to absently rub the outline of the growing erection in his pants.

As he thought about it, he realized that they had actually not had sex since last Saturday morning in the hotel. Having so completely relieved themselves from their sexual cravings Friday night, they had no cravings all the way through to Tuesday, which is when they officially went on their abstinence diet. Startled, Mark heard the doorbell ring. He quickly glanced over at the clock on the wall. It was 8:25PM. Mark got up and headed towards the door.

Mark opened the door to see Ty standing there holding a bottle of wine in one hand. Mark said with a smile, "Hey. Come on in," as he motioned Ty into the room.

Mark then asked, "What's this?" as he looked down at the bottle of wine Ty was holding.

Ty answered, "I'm not sure but I think it's the same bottle Destiny brought to the hotel room," as he handed the bottle over to Mark and walked into the room.

Mark said, "Thanks. I'm sure Destiny will love it."

After an awkward moment of silence Mark asked, "So. Did you find the house OK?"

Ty answered, "Yeah, I looked it up on MapQuest beforehand."

Mark replied, "Good," as he began to feel a little uncomfortable again and started searching his mind for things to talk about.

Ty glanced around the room and then offered, "You guys have a beautiful home," as he continued to take it in.

Mark responded, "Thanks," and then added, "Can I get you something to drink?"

Ty glanced down at the bottle he brought and then asked, "Actually...What do you have?"

Mark answered enthusiastically, "Everything!"

Ty thought for a moment and then asked, "Bourbon?"

Mark replied, "On the rocks with Coke?"

Ty answered, "Just on the rocks is fine."

Mark turned toward the kitchen to make Ty's drink just as Destiny walked out of the bedroom and into the living room with her wine glass in hand.

Ty was following Mark into the kitchen when he saw Destiny out of the corner of his eye walk into the living room. Ty stopped, turned and with a wide grin forming on his face, said charmingly to Destiny in his usual deep voice, "Well, hello beautiful."

Hearing this, Mark stopped and turned to see Destiny. She looked sexier than he had ever seen her before and Mark knew tonight was going to be an incredible night.

Destiny felt herself start to melt as she remembered how sexy Ty's voice was. A wide smile spread across her face as she caught herself responding naughtily to Ty, "Hey, sexy."

Mark was standing halfway into the kitchen observing their exchange and watched as Ty began to make his way slowly towards Destiny.

Destiny met him halfway into the living room, putting her glass down on the table beside her. She held her arms out and the two embraced each other.

After a long moment, they released each other. Mark heard Ty ask her something in a soft voice that Mark could not quite make out. Destiny's face was very close to Ty's as he spoke and Mark saw Destiny beginning to blush and then grinning very naughtily, she looked up into his eyes and answered in a soft, barely audible voice, "Yeah." Ty leaned into Destiny and they began to kiss softly.

Mark watched momentarily as they held each other kissing and felt a cool rippling sensation flow over his body. He wondered what Ty had said to Destiny to cause her to blush so much. With a wide smile fixed to his face, Mark forced himself to turn away from this beautiful scene to give them a little privacy.

Mark walked over to the bar in the corner of the kitchen and proceeded to make Ty's drink. With his back turned to them, Mark imagined the scene unfolding behind him. Mark could hear that they were not talking, which meant they must still be kissing each other, and the silence went on for a while.

He thought it strange that he could find it almost as arousing to watch them make-out as he did by not watching them make-out but knowing that they were. The two sensations felt very different from each other but both were a huge turn-on to him. Right now he was enjoying the 'not watching them make-out but knowing that they were' sensation.

Finished making Ty's drink, Mark couldn't bear not being able to watch them any longer, so he turned to see what he was missing.

He found Destiny leading Ty to the couch in the living room. She sat beside Ty as Mark arrived with his drink and handed it to him. Mark chose to sit in the leather chair across the table from them.

Ty took a sip of his glass and put it on the coffee table. Turning back to Destiny, he said charmingly, "Well, you look gorgeous tonight," and then added, "I recognize the dress," as he smiled at her.

Destiny had to think for a moment. *How could he recognize this dress? I haven't worn it for him before...* then with sudden realization she said, "Oh!" and then added grinning, "So, do you still have my picture?"

Ty answered simply, "I do," as he produced his own grin.

Destiny reached for her glass resting on the coffee table next to Ty's, took a sip and then returned it to the table. Destiny leaned back and turned towards Ty.

Destiny found herself glancing down reminiscently at the bulge in his pants, she looked up again into Ty's face and found herself suddenly at a loss for words and decided to look down again. She momentarily felt ashamed of herself, as she couldn't seem to take her eyes off of it.

As she looked at his crotch she felt her hand uncontrollably sliding over and reaching for Ty's bulge as if her hand had a mind of its own. Her hand came to a rest on his bulge and she looked up at Ty's face seeking his permission. Ty was grinning as he reached over to put his arm around her, which told her she had permission.

Then she looked down at his bulge again and watched as her hand began to probe.

She felt his hardness growing in the confined space and grasped the now distinctly bent shaft pushing up against his pants. She wanted to release it from its cage as she looked up again into his face and asked with her eyes, 'May I?'

Not willing to wait for permission this time, she looked down again at what her hand was gripping and felt herself slowly sliding sideways off the couch and onto her knees. She looked up again into Ty's face seeking his approval and upon receiving it, back down at his pants again. Destiny began to unbutton his pants and pull down his zipper as Ty removed his shirt.

She grabbed his pants and briefs as one, as she did before, and began to pull down as Ty lifted his body slightly to free them. They came down over his knees and then down to his ankles. Destiny could see Ty's cock standing straight up and she grew sopping wet at the sight.

Destiny now took her time removing Ty's shoes from his feet while she sat there on the floor below him.

Mark was unable to see everything Destiny was doing on the floor at Ty's feet so he leaned forward in his chair and quietly pulled the coffee table back away from the couch. Still not liking the view from his angle, he chose to relocate himself to the chair at the end of the coffee table. Sitting down, Mark began to unconsciously rub the outline of his now semi-erect penis through his pants.

Mark watched as Destiny continued to delicately, slowly remove Ty's clothing like an obedient servant. It almost seemed like she was trying to tease Ty. Destiny set aside his shoes and socks neatly under the coffee table. Occasionally, Destiny would glance up into Ty's face seeking his continued approval momentarily before returning her attention to the task of removing his clothing. She proceeded to delicately remove his pants and, with attention to detail, she folded them nicely before putting them on the edge of the coffee table. She looked up at Ty's face seeking his approval with the job she had done before proceeding to do the same with his briefs.

With his clothing now neatly put away, Destiny gently spread Ty's knees as she positioned herself slowly in between them. She looked up into his face once more as her hands wrapped around Ty's fully erect cock.

Destiny leaned forward, opened her mouth and fed Ty into it.

Mark watched as Destiny stuffed Ty into her mouth and her head began to move slowly up and down in short stokes. He noticed now how much she admired Ty's huge throbbing cock as she handled it so delicately and with reverence.

After awhile, Mark saw Destiny pause for a moment and with Ty's cock still in her mouth; she slowly sank her shoulders down low between Ty's legs. As she did so, Destiny tilted her head back as far as she could and then Mark watched with amazement as Destiny began to swallow Ty from a horizontal position.

Destiny, having found the correct position now based on her experimentation and secret practice sessions the past week, took a deep breath and held it as she began to force Ty's cock deep down her throat. Ty reacted by throwing his head back and moaning in pleasure.

Mark watched as he saw Destiny starting to gag but was surprised to see her not stopping but instead going deeper, swallowing even more of Ty. Mark was reminded of a sword swallower.

Mark began to stroke himself roughly through his pants as he watched Destiny force Ty's cock slowly down her throat until she had taken in all of him.

Unable to control her gag reflex any longer, Destiny suddenly pulled Ty all the way back out.

Destiny leaned back and began to cough uncontrollably while she fought back laughter at the same time.

Ty said forcefully, "Don't stop."

Destiny, sensing the urgency in his command, immediately regained control over herself, leaned over, took a deep breath and put his cock back in her mouth as she pulled herself down between his legs and fed his cock deep into her mouth again from this odd horizontal position.

She held it there as long as she could then pulled it back out to catch her breath. Her eyes were watering profusely now as she wiped the tears from her face. Again, she took a deep breath before swallowing Ty whole, held it there, and then pulled it back out.

Destiny continued this a few more times before she found a rhythm that enabled her to swallow Ty completely, retract him partially, then breath through her nose before swallowing him completely again.

Soon after, Ty put his hand on the back of Destiny's head and began to thrust his cock down Destiny's throat at a faster rate. Destiny struggled to keep up and eventually adapted to the faster rate by holding her breath in between several strokes.

Mark began to notice a change in Ty's moans and then he realized that Ty was cumming down Destiny's throat.

Mark could see that Ty wasn't completely erect anymore and he seemed to bypass the sudden rock hard erection a man would normally get at climax.

Instead, Ty seemed to be cumming a little bit every time Destiny went deep on him.

Destiny began to drool cum from the side of her mouth as Ty continued to thrust his cock deep down her throat.

Mark was unable to take it anymore and he quickly pulled his penis out of his pants and stroked it vigorously until he came all over himself.

Ty's climax went on for a while and when Ty finally released Destiny's head, Destiny continued to nurse and swallow Ty's cum from his cock until he had no more to give. Eventually, she pulled Ty out of her mouth, leaned back and began to laugh as she wiped tears from her eyes and face.

Finally, she asked, with a sense of pride in her voice, "How did you like that?" as she grinned up into Ty's face.

Ty, who seemed completely drained, responded approvingly, "You're the first woman I've met who could that."

Destiny was very pleased with herself indeed as she announced cheerfully, "I've been practicing."

Ty replied, "Apparently so!"

Mark was wondering how she was able to do that too and it occurred to him then that she must have been secretly practicing this past week. Mark remembered now how he had occasionally heard Destiny coughing in their home office as he watched TV in the other room.

Destiny often used their office computer to play games as she unwound from the day's work while Mark watched TV. Mark had noticed at the time her coughs seemed a little strange as if she had accidentally swallowed her drink wrong. Mark would holler to her, "Are you alright?" and after a moment she would respond, "I'm fine." Mark had dismissed these coughs without thinking much of it. Also, Mark remembered that she had been eating a lot of bananas the past week. But now, as he thought about it she wasn't just eating the bananas, she was "practicing" with them.

Ty's cell phone rang. He reached for it on the coffee table and as he looked to see who was calling a surprised look came over his face. He answered it.

"Hey you! How are you?" Ty said excitedly as Mark and Destiny watched.

The call dragged on for a while and eventually Destiny stood up to go to the bathroom. Mark got up and went over to the stereo to turn the music down. Mark and Destiny puttered around the house looking for things to do as they waited for Ty to finish the call.

As they did, Destiny began to wonder if the evening's activities had already come to an end. She found herself jealous of the person on the other end of the line as she could tell by the way Ty was talking that he was speaking to a female friend.

Eventually, Ty ended the call.

He turned to Destiny and said, "Sorry about that. That was an old friend I haven't talked to in a long time."

Destiny dismissed it saying, "Oh. That's fine. I understand," as she sat down again next to Ty on the couch.

Mark was in the kitchen making himself a drink.

Destiny expected that Ty wasn't ready for more just yet and was even preparing herself for Ty to call it a night when Ty put his arm around Destiny and asked, "So. Where were we?" as he smiled into her eyes.

Destiny, surprised, felt herself getting wet again as she searched for words. Before she could say anything, Ty leaned into her and the two began kissing again.

Mark was about to return to the living room when he noticed Ty and Destiny on the couch kissing. Mark, too, thought that the evening was coming to an early end and was surprised to see them passionately kissing on the couch. Mark didn't want to intrude and risk interrupting them so he looked for reasons to stay in the kitchen.

Occasionally, Mark would peek around the corner to find them on the couch still making-out. Destiny was now lying on the couch with her head leaning back on the armrest as Ty lay gently on top of her kissing her deeply while they probed each other's bodies.

After a few minutes, Mark quietly made his way back to one of the chairs trying not to distract them as he sat down to watch.

Mark watched as Ty began removing Destiny's dress. She leaned forward to let him pull the zipper down the back. As Ty tried to remove her dress they were discouraged at not being able to remove it completely without disrupting their kissing and they gave up removing it for the moment. Destiny leaned back once again resting her head on the armrest of the couch.

They resumed their passionate kissing for several more minutes before Destiny whispered into Ty's ear, "Do you want me to get on top of you?"

Ty nodded approval.

Destiny stood up and finished removing her dress. Now she was only wearing her corset, stockings, high-heel boots and a choke chain as she stood before Ty.

Destiny straddled Ty's legs as she made her way up onto his lap.

She leaned forward and found that she had to lift one leg up onto her foot in order to get the height she needed for Ty's fully erect cock to fit in between her legs.

Ty guided his cock to the entrance of Destiny's pussy as she began to lower herself onto it. The head of Ty's cock began to press hard against her opening as she allowed more and more of her weight to bear down on him. Finally, Destiny felt Ty suddenly enter her and she let out a loud gasp in response.

Destiny had to take a moment to get use to his enormous girth again before she could continue. Eventually, she carefully lowered her leg so that she was resting on both knees and proceeded to slowly lower herself further down taking Ty deeper inside her.

It took some time for Destiny to accept Ty all the way inside her. As she worked it in deeper, Mark watched from the chair he was sitting in with a look of astonishment on his face. Mark continued to be amazed at how big Ty was and that Destiny was able to take so much of him inside her. Mark began to rub his penis through his pants again.

Eventually, Destiny came to rest delicately on Ty's lap with Ty fully inserted in her. She took a deep breath and then leaned forward to kiss Ty. They kissed each other passionately for just a moment before Destiny pulled herself away. Then as Destiny stared into Ty's eyes, she began to carefully lean back. Her eyes closed again and she began to make a quivering sound as Ty slid even deeper inside her. A moment later, Destiny began a slow rhythmic movement up and down on Ty.

Mark watched in awe as Destiny rode Ty. He had unzipped his pants and had his hand down there absently stroking himself but sometimes he stopped stroking himself altogether as he became lost in the sheer beauty of seeing Destiny ride that magnificent cock.

Destiny's rhythm slowly increased in intensity over time and after several minutes, she began to moan uncontrollably as she felt her first orgasm of the night.

Minutes later, she was riding Ty fervently as she had another orgasm.

Over time, Destiny's legs started to get tired from riding Ty so hard and she began to slow her rhythm as they focused more on kissing. Eventually, exhausted, her rhythm stopped all together.

They embraced each other and gently kissed with Destiny resting on his lap and with Ty still inserted deep inside her. A few minutes later Destiny whispered into Ty's ear, "Do you want to move to the bedroom?"

Ty grinned and nodded in agreement.

Destiny slowly removed Ty from deep inside her and climbed off him.

Destiny stumbled a little as she tried to stand up and fell back down on Ty. Ty responded by catching her as she fell. Destiny felt a little embarrassed at her clumsy dismount and said laughingly as Ty still held her, "Sorry, I guess I wasn't quite ready to stand up yet."

Ty released her and said, "No problem." And then added teasingly, "Shall I carry you to the bedroom?"

Destiny laughed and said, "Thanks. But, I think I can make it on my own."

Standing before him now, Destiny reached out for Ty's hand and began to lead him to the master bedroom. Mark quickly zipped his pants up and followed them in. Though they were the only ones in the house, Mark felt compelled to close the door behind him as if he needed to hide their debauchery from the rest of the house.

In the bedroom now, Ty and Destiny stood beside the bed kissing again as Mark quietly took a seat in a chair he had strategically set in the corner of the room earlier in the day. Mark thought with some amusement when he was putting the chair there that if things go well, he might be spending a lot of nights sitting in that chair masturbating to the lewd activities his wife and another man would be engaged in right before his very own eyes.

As they kissed, Ty gently laid Destiny down on the bed as he climbed on top of her and positioned himself between her legs.

Destiny lay there expectantly as Ty began to guide his still throbbing cock inside her.

Mark watched from his chair as they started to make love. Ty thrusted Destiny with a slow and gentle motion at first and Mark could see by the look on her face that she was already starting to cum again as she made a soft moaning sound. But Ty's thrusts were already beginning to increase in vigor and ferocity.

With each passing minute, Ty began to thrust Destiny harder and harder until eventually, Ty seemed to be fucking Destiny as hard as he could as he held her firmly by her hips. Then Mark was completely stunned to see Ty summon even more strength as he began to fuck Destiny harder still.

Destiny, who had been suspiciously quiet until now, suddenly let out a terrifying scream that immediately caused Mark to jump out of his chair and rush over to save her. Mark arrived at the side of the bed to find Destiny desperately trying to squirm away from Ty's thrusts. But Ty seemed to have a death grip on Destiny by her hips as he continued to relentlessly pound his cock deep inside her. Mark looked on as Destiny let out another scream. Neither Destiny nor Ty seemed to be aware of Mark's presence at the edge of the bed and he wasn't sure what to do. His instincts told him he should try to help her but Mark remembered the last weekend when he got up to intervene and how Destiny shook her head urging him not to. Mark wasn't sure at what point he was supposed to do something. Instead, he stood there helplessly watching Destiny trying to free herself from Ty's grip.

Eventually, Mark saw Destiny begin to relax a little as she gave up on trying to free herself. Mark watched as her whole body shuddered violently with each of Ty's thrusts but Destiny seemed more willing to take it now. It seemed as if she was beginning to resign herself to whatever pain Ty expected her to endure.

As Mark stood there, he still wondered if he should be doing something to stop this before she got seriously hurt. Mark considered telling Ty to ease off a bit but he seemed to be lost in some kind of sexual frenzy and Mark knew he wouldn't be able to get his attention so easily. Mark even considered trying to pull Ty off of Destiny but he knew the grip he had on her hips was unshakable.

As Mark contemplated his options he began to hear Destiny make that pain/pleasure sound again that he remembered from the hotel room. Mark also recognized the look on Destiny's face. He saw that she was starting to get control of the pain, which meant she would soon start experiencing an uncontrollable series of orgasms.

Mark was suddenly on his knees beside the bed. Mark reached out and grasped Destiny's hand, which was clenching a fistful of bed sheeting. Destiny, who was suddenly aware of Mark's presence beside the bed, released the bed sheets and grabbed Mark's hand. She squeezed it hard as she fought to overcome the pain of Ty's powerful thrusts. Mark stroked his penis vigorously with the other hand as Mark and Destiny looked into each other's eyes lovingly. Ty's thrusts continued mercilessly.

They both knew that Ty was lost in his own throes of passion and that neither of them could stop him now even if they wanted to.

As Destiny squeezed Mark's hand he began to cum uncontrollably all over the side of the bed as he pulled on his penis violently.

Destiny, with the pain and pleasure look on her face could only gaze understandingly into Mark's eyes as he writhed in ecstasy. Mark continued to pull hard on his penis until finally exhausted, he laid his head down on the edge of the bed.

Without notice, Ty suddenly pulled himself out of Destiny and roughly rolled her over and on to her knees.

Destiny had to let go of Mark's hand in the process.

Ty firmly mounted Destiny from behind and using his rock-solid grip on her waist, he began to, once again, fuck her as hard as he could.

Destiny had to scream in pain again until she got used to this new position but this time her screams quickly faded.

Mark helplessly pulled on his cum covered penis beside the bed as he looked up at them. Destiny was crying now, he noticed, and he could see tears streaming down her face as Ty continued slamming her pussy from behind now. Mark desperately reached out and grasped her forearm to comfort her as it was all he could do for her right now.

Mark understood that this was what Destiny had wanted; what she had been needing for so long. And as much as it was hurting her, Mark knew that the more it hurt her now, the more powerful her orgasms would be when they finally came.

Yet despite knowing this, Mark couldn't help but to feel a little ashamed of himself as he stood by doing nothing as his wife cried out in pain from the relentless pounding Ty was giving her.

Mark eventually lowered his head in disgrace, unable to look at his wife's teary face any longer, and began to unabashedly stroke his penis again.

Slowly, Destiny began to regain her control over the pain and then after a few more minutes, she was suddenly and unexpectedly seized by a powerfully intense orgasm. Her eyes suddenly went wide and her whole body seemed to go rigid for a moment as she was seized by one orgasm after another.

Minutes later, Ty groaned loudly as he finally erupted deep inside her.

When they had finished, Mark was still lost, again, as he continued to mindlessly pull on his penis, ejaculating continuously while he held Destiny's forearm.

He was dimly aware that he had never experienced an orgasm as intense or as long as he did when he watched Destiny in this condition with Ty.

Ty was now resting over Destiny's back as he breathed heavily. Ty seemed thoroughly exhausted as he tried to catch his breath.

Destiny was trying to catch her breath too as Mark noticed that they had both worked up quite a sweat.

Eventually, Ty began to rise off of Destiny and Mark became aware that the show was over for now as he tried to drag himself back to reality. He was surprised to see that it was already 11:00PM as he stood up and returned to his chair to cover himself.

Ty pulled himself out of Destiny and the two lay down next to each other on the bed, exhausted.

Eventually, Destiny got up and went to the bathroom. She returned with a wet towel and proceeded to clean Ty's cock for him. Ty said, "Thanks."

Destiny smiled as she lay down on his chest and the two playfully kissed.

After awhile, Ty looked over and said to Mark, "I could really use a glass of water," and Destiny piped in, "Me, too!"

Mark got up out of his chair in the corner and went to the kitchen to fetch everybody a glass of water.

Mark found himself taking his time about it. Mark thought, *maybe if I give them a little time alone they might start getting into it again.* Mark hoped so as he was already starting to feel a little aroused again as he envisioned them going at it once more.

Several minutes later, Mark returned with three glasses of ice water. As he walked into the room he noticed the two talking quietly as Destiny lay on her forearms looking up into Ty's face.

They stopped talking as soon as they saw Mark entering the room. Mark handed them the glasses and they took them appreciatively.

Finally, Ty, grinning, asked Mark, "So you like to watch?"

Destiny playfully hit Ty and said smiling, "Stop. That's mean."

Mark's face went red as he admitted, "Yeah. So?"

Ty replied, "No. I don't mean there is anything wrong with that or anything… I was just wondering what you get out of it."

Mark answered honestly, "I don't know exactly… It's just a big turn-on to me."

Ty simply nodded his head and didn't press the issue further.

Eventually, Destiny said, "I wish we could have some music in here," as she looked over to Mark questioningly.

Mark got the hint and went out to the living room and unplugged the laptop computer from the stereo and brought it into the bedroom.

As Mark setup the music, Destiny and Ty began teasingly and playfully kissing each other again.

Before Mark could sit down again, Destiny asked if he could refill her glass of water. Mark returned with two glasses of water, one was for Ty.

Mark sat back down in the chair in the corner of the room and watched as Destiny and Ty went back to playfully kissing each other.

Occasionally, they would pause as they took a drink of water from their glasses. They would start to flirt with each other a little bit and then return to kissing.

After awhile, Mark felt as if they had completely forgotten about him as he quietly sat in the corner watching them. Mark became transfixed as he watched them flirt and playfully kiss each other, completely uninhibited by his presence and it was extremely arousing to watch. It was almost as if he was watching TV and absently played with himself as the story unfolded before him.

Mark found he was very relaxed and comfortable now and he was thoroughly enjoying the pornographic nature of Ty and Destiny making-out on the bed.

They had stopped for a moment and seemed to be talking so that Mark couldn't actually hear what they were saying. After a moment, Destiny turned to face Mark and asked pleadingly, "Honey?" she smiled before continuing, "Would you be OK with going into the other room for awhile?"

Mark suddenly felt very conspicuous and he had to take a moment to gather himself before he could consider Destiny's request.

Mark started, "Umm. I guess so..."

Destiny added imploringly, "It would just be for a little while... I promise."

Mark contemplated.

Finally she added, "Please?"

Destiny's eyes pleaded with Mark and he found himself giving in to her request as he stood up and began exit the room.

As Mark reached the door, Destiny said, "Thanks Hun... I promise we won't be too long."

Mark smiled at her and said graciously, "No problem. Take as much time as you need," as he closed the door behind him.

Mark could sympathize with Destiny's request but he couldn't help but feel like he was a little child being sent to his room so the grown ups could have some naughty time. As Mark sat on the couch, he could hear them talking again in the bedroom and he started to feel a little left out of the fun. Mark decided he should watch some TV just to kill some time but he found himself putting one of their interracial videos in the DVD player instead.

It didn't take long for Mark to be distracted from the two of them in the other room as he watched Lexington Steele pounding away on some tiny brunette. But after several minutes of watching, it suddenly came back to him and he felt a jolt of arousal as he remembered that his wife and her black lover were actually in the bedroom just down the hall from where he was. That unlike this make believe DVD he was watching, his wife and her black stud were going at it for real, right now, this very minute and just a few feet away from him! Mark considered all the naughty things they could be doing in there this very moment and his heart raced with excitement.

It had been at least half an hour since he left them alone together in the bedroom and Mark couldn't take it anymore. Mark got up and tiptoed over to the closed bedroom door. He held his ear to the door and could hear them whispering to each other but he couldn't quite make out what they were saying.

Mark listened as it grew silent for a moment and all Mark could hear was the music coming from the laptop computer.

Then Mark heard Destiny make a gasping noise. A moment later he heard them whispering again. He still couldn't quite make out what they were saying and then he heard Destiny say in a clear, slightly louder voice, "I think you need to put a little more lubrication on. That's why."

Mark wondered, *just what exactly are they up to in there?* Mark could only think of one reason why they would need lubrication but knowing the size of Ty's cock, he was unwilling to believe it.

Mark listened as it grew quite again. He strained to hold his ear against the door. The music was playing and Mark couldn't hear any other sounds for a couple of minutes.

And then suddenly, as clear as day, he heard Destiny gasp loudly and almost simultaneously he heard Ty begin to moan followed by Destiny letting out a slow breathy moan that sounded like "Ahhhhhhh." Her moan trailed off for a moment then it was abruptly cut off as she gasped again.

Then Mark heard Ty speak words of encouragement in a very comforting tone, he said, "There you go. I told you, you could do it."

Mark could hear Destiny reluctantly respond, "Uh Huh," as she fought off another gasp.

Then Mark could hear Destiny urgently plead, "Wait!" and then a moment later she whispered, "Just hold it there for a moment. OK?"

Mark could hear Destiny breathing in and out rhythmically with a sound that reminded Mark of someone getting ready to lift something heavy. She would take a deep a breath, hold it and then exhale with a breathy sound.

After awhile, her breathing faded and then he heard Destiny say with a touch of pain in her voice, "OK...You can push it in a little further," before urgently adding, "But go slow!"

Mark heard Destiny gasp loudly again before she started the same deep rhythmic breathing.

After a while, Mark began to hear a slow rhythmic creaking coming from their bed. It began to pick up pace until it eventually kept time with her breathing.

Mark had become completely erect by this time as he stood with his ear to the door and he wanted to stroke his penis right there but he was concerned that they might hear him through the door.

Mark reluctantly tiptoed back to the couch and began stroking himself as he imagined what Ty was actually doing to his wife in their bedroom.

Mark quickly came in his hand and shortly after, he unexpectedly fell asleep with his hand wrapped around his penis.

Much later, Mark was startled awake to the sound of their bedroom door opening. He looked over to see Destiny in her silk robe peering out at him. She smiled and whispered, "Just checking on you."

Destiny took a quick glance back behind her before she decided to race out and give Mark a quick update. She whispered, "We're finished. Ty's just in the bathroom now getting dressed. He'll be leaving soon and then you can come in. OK?"

Mark nodded as she ran back into the room and closed the door behind her. Mark thought she was acting very mischievously. Mark couldn't remember the last time he had seen her like that. Mark tried to sit up straight and he glanced over to the clock on the wall to see what time it was. It was 1:38AM and Mark wondered just how much he must have missed.

Mark pulled his pants up and made his way to the kitchen to wash up and get a drink of water. As he stood before the sink, Mark heard the bedroom door open again. Mark walked towards the living room and met Ty and Destiny there. She was showing Ty to the door.

Ty opened the front door and began to walk out when Destiny grabbed him by the arm and he swung around to face her again. Destiny walked into Ty's arms and the two began to kiss in the doorway.

They held the kiss for awhile before finally, they released each other and Ty walked out. Destiny closed the door behind him. Mark briefly thought, *I hope the neighbors weren't watching.*

Destiny wordlessly walked towards Mark and embraced him tightly. They kissed for a moment before she pulled away and said to Mark, "Thanks for giving us some alone time. I promise to make it up to you somehow."

Mark smiled dismissively and asked, "Did you have a good time?"

Destiny had a broad smile across her face as she nodded.

Then she added, "I love you."

Mark could see she was very sincere. *She must have had a really good time tonight.*

She held him tightly again as Mark said, "I love you, too."

Destiny led Mark to their bedroom and the two quickly fell asleep.

Chapter 7: Unexpected Guests

The next Monday night, Destiny was unwinding from work when she received a call from an old friend of hers. Destiny had worked in the same office with Megan at Destiny's old company. Megan was much younger than Destiny and she always came to Destiny for relationship advice. Shortly after Destiny left the company she received a call from Megan announcing that she and her boyfriend were getting married and she asked Destiny to be the maid of honor. Destiny was busy at her new job and she didn't know how she was going to find the time but she agreed anyway.

Destiny had only talked with Megan a few times after the wedding as the two drifted apart. Now, eight months later, she was surprised to get a call from her. Megan announced that she and Eric were getting a divorce and she wanted to know if she could stay with them for a short while as she looked for an apartment to move into.

Destiny felt imposed upon but she knew that Megan didn't have any family close by and she could sense the desperation in her voice. Mark and Destiny had a spare bedroom she could stay in so Destiny finally conceded to Megan's request.

Destiny knew that Megan had a tendency to be naïve about relationships so she wasn't too surprised to learn that their marriage hadn't lasted long. Megan was very beautiful, Destiny remembered, and she had a young girl's innocence about her that caused men to gush over her.

Megan moved into Mark and Destiny's spare bedroom that night. Mark remembered Destiny staying up and comforting Megan that first night until the early morning hours as Megan cried in her arms.

Destiny had learned that Megan had caught Eric cheating on her and over the next couple of weeks, Megan began to confess to Destiny everything that had happened.

Destiny discovered that their problems started shortly after they were married. Megan had said it all started one night when they had a few friends over. They all had a lot to drink and eventually everyone had left except one of Megan's girlfriends, Jessica. Megan had gone to the bathroom and when she returned she found Eric dancing in the living room with Jessica. Megan could see Eric's hand resting on Jessica's behind as they danced closely with each other. Megan thought that Jessica was a little bit of a floozy and she didn't completely trust her with Eric. Jessica was a little older than Megan and she was much more experienced than Megan. Megan had learned this one time as Jessica shared some of her shocking sexual escapades with her. Megan liked Jessica but she thought she could never to do some of the things that Jessica had done and she certainly wouldn't admit it to anyone if she had.

Eric looked over at Megan as she stood there watching and winked at her as he began to grind himself against her friend. Megan stormed off to their bedroom. A short while later, Eric came into the bedroom and seeing she was unhappy, he asked, "What's the matter baby?"

Megan didn't respond.

Eric said, "I was just thinking we could have a little fun together... Just the three of us."

Megan was shocked. She couldn't believe that Eric was suggesting that she would be interested in having a threesome and suspected that Eric was just looking for an excuse to have sex with her friend. Finally she asked angrily, "And what gave you that idea?"

Eric explained, "I just thought... It might be a little fun to... try something different."

Megan said heatedly, "Hmmm," as she crossed her arms and pouted at him.

Eric continued, "I thought maybe you might like it… if you gave it a try."

Megan didn't say anything as she sat their angrily sulking. Finally, Eric said frustrated, "Ok. I'm sorry. We don't have to do anything if you don't want to."

Eric sat down next to Megan on the bed and put his arm around her. She wouldn't look at him for a long while as Eric continued to apologize to her. Eventually, Megan's anger subsided and he was able to convince her to return to the living room. Jessica was gathering her things and preparing to leave. Eric tried to convince her to stay for a while longer but she just smiled and said, "Maybe next time," as she looked over at Megan and winked at her.

Megan began to blush as she realized that Jessica had been plotting a threesome with her and Eric all night and that's why she had stuck around after everyone else had left. *She was trying to seduce my husband,* she thought.

Megan suddenly found herself getting a little turned on but she quickly suppressed those feelings as she told herself, 'that's just wrong,' and she convinced herself it really was.

Megan continued to be friendly with Jessica after that night but she held her at a distance and would never invite her over again.

Over the next few weeks, Megan noticed that Eric was always trying to talk her into having a threesome, especially while they were having sex, and each time she would emphatically tell him no. She wondered, *what's wrong with him?* Eventually, Eric stopped trying.

Things seem to return to normal for a while but then Megan began to notice that Eric seemed to be losing interest in her. He would get frustrated and annoyed with her easily. She noticed he didn't want to have sex as much as he used to either and when they did have sex; it was less passionate than it used to be.

Megan and Eric struggled with their marriage over the next few months. Eric started going out more with his friends and sometimes he would come home very late. That's when Megan started to suspect that he might be having an affair. Megan tried to keep a close tab on Eric when he went out. She would make up reasons to call him while he was with his friends but she could never catch him in the act.

Then one day, she came home from work early. It was only lunchtime but she had a headache and decided to take the rest of the day off. Megan remembered that Eric had taken the day off to run some errands and so she wasn't expecting to find him at home.

Megan went to unlock the door to their apartment and found it already unlocked. She walked in and closed the door behind her.

She was about to call out to Eric when she heard voices coming from their bedroom. Megan, perplexed, quietly walked over to the bedroom door. She felt anger already building inside her and as she peered through the open door, she was shocked at what she actually saw.

Megan saw a woman straddling a man while another man mounted her from behind. She didn't recognize the man behind the woman but the man on the bottom was Eric.

Megan was speechless as she stood there. The woman was moaning in deep pleasure as the man behind her rocked her rhythmically back and forth. Megan was shocked further when she discovered the man behind her was fucking her in the ass while Eric had his cock shoved in her pussy. For a brief moment, Megan envied the condition this woman was in and she began to feel aroused. Megan was transfixed as she gazed upon them.

Finally, Eric noticed her. Eric eyes grew wide and he began to struggle out from beneath this woman as he shouted, "Megan!"

The other two looked her way. That's when Megan recognized the woman. *Jessica!*

Megan was filled with rage as Eric tried desperately to explain. Megan glared at the other two as they quickly got dressed and vacated the premises.

Finally, Megan shouted, "How could you?" as tears began to roll down her cheeks.

Later that night, Megan moved in to Mark and Destiny's guest room.

Over the next few days, Mark found himself trying to stay away from home as it seemed Megan was constantly prone to sudden outbursts of tears. Destiny had to comfort her through these times and they talked for hours in the guest room.

Destiny could understand why Megan was so upset. She thought, *if I ever caught Mark cheating, I don't know what I would do.* But Destiny understood that this happened a lot in unhappy marriages. Eventually, one or the other will stray. But sometimes they work things out. Divorce isn't the only option. Destiny wondered why Megan didn't see the warning signs that were clearly there. Obviously, Eric wasn't getting his sexual needs fulfilled by Megan and it was just a matter of time before....

Destiny knew that Megan was too young and inexperienced to know how to deal with Eric's 'unconventional' sexual desires. But Megan had married him (presumably because she truly loved Eric), which meant she had some obligation to at least try and work through their problems. Even if Megan wasn't open to sexual experimentation, Destiny thought she should have made an effort to somehow meet him half way.

Once Eric found out where Megan was staying, he somehow got Destiny's cell phone number and started to call Destiny on a regular basis. He would plead with her to tell Megan how sorry he was and that he really loved her and wanted to make it up to her somehow. Destiny didn't particularly like being put in the middle of these two but she decided that unless Eric was prone to habitual infidelity, there might be a chance to save their marriage and that she would at least give it a try.

Destiny knew that Megan thought highly of her and with her guidance, Destiny thought she might get Megan to give Eric a second chance. She also knew that in order for it to last, Eric needed to learn how to share his needs with Megan so the two could find a way to work things out.

Destiny started by explaining Eric's side to Megan. She explained that although Eric was wrong to assume that she would automatically be interested in a threesome and he should have discussed it with her before the night of the party, he was clearly trying to share his desires with her in the days that followed. Destiny explained how Megan should have been more open to discussing what he wanted from her and because she wasn't, Eric began to look outside their marriage to fulfill his sexual desires. What Eric did was wrong, Destiny explained, but Megan didn't do anything to help prevent that from happening either.

Eventually, Megan began to forgive Eric for his indiscretion as Destiny began to convince her that she had made some mistakes in their relationship, too.

One night while Mark was working late, the two talked alone in Megan's room about how to patch up her marriage to Eric.

Megan and Destiny sat next to each other on the edge of the bed as Destiny began to explain that if she wanted to keep the fire alive in her relationship with Eric then she would need to broaden herself and be more open to trying new things.

Megan asked, "What about you and Mark?"

Destiny offered, "We have our own things that we do to keep our sex life exciting," while withholding an I-have-a-secret smile. Destiny also had to make a conscious effort to keep from blushing.

Megan asked excitedly, "Really? Like what?"

Destiny replied, "Oh… Just things."

Destiny didn't feel Megan could handle the idea that there was a whole interracial hotwifing community out there and that they had become a part of it. Or that Destiny liked getting fucked hard by a big black guy and that Mark liked to watch her getting fucked while he jerked-off in the corner. No, Megan was too innocent to learn about that kind of stuff… yet.

Instead, Destiny offered, "Just know that having a threesome with your husband might not be the naughtiest thing you guys will ever end up doing together."

Megan seemed to be relieved to hear that it is was OK for a married woman to be naughty.

Finally, she said, "Really? Because Eric said the only reason he had slept with Jessica is because he knew she would be willing to do things; naughty things, that I wouldn't do."

Destiny replied, "See? There you go."

Megan looked thoughtful for a moment before she said, "I can be naughty."

She continued excitedly, "I have naughty thoughts!" she exclaimed.

Destiny laughed at Megan's excitement for realizing that she had naughty thoughts. *She seems so cute and innocent sometimes*, Destiny thought.

Finally, Destiny asked cheerfully, "Like what?"

Megan looked into Destiny's face and grew quiet for a moment.

Suddenly and without warning, Megan leaned into Destiny and began kissing her.

Destiny was stunned. Her eyes closed as she found herself instinctively kissing Megan back. Destiny contemplated how she could decline Megan's advances without rejecting her and hurting Megan's already fragile self-esteem and as she considered this, Destiny began to notice just how soft and sensuous Megan's lips felt pressed against hers.

Several seconds had passed and once Megan began groping Destiny's body, Destiny found herself reciprocating as her hand unconsciously slid up Megan's shirt, under her bra and over her soft, warm breast. Megan moaned her approval. They began to kiss more deeply and groped each other with urgency.

Several more seconds went by before Destiny's better judgment began to reassert itself and she reluctantly began to pull away from Megan.

Destiny couldn't help but to feel she was somehow taking advantage of this sweet and innocent girl who was going through a personal crisis in her life right now and therefore was prone to poor judgment and impulsive behavior. Destiny knew that Megan trusted and depended on her for guidance, especially now, and that it would be up to Destiny to be the responsible adult in the room and put a stop to this before Megan did something she could end up regretting later.

Megan looked back feeling confused and rejected and asked, "What's the matter? This is OK isn't it?"

Destiny desperately wanted to say yes but instead she tried to explain, "I'm sorry. I can't… I just don't want to take advantage of you right now, OK?"

Megan, head held down, pouted thoughtfully for a moment and said, "But… What if… I want you to… take advantage of me?"

Destiny was unsure of what to say. Megan seemed so vulnerable and unsure of herself as she tried to explain, "I just always dreamed of you…of us… maybe someday…you know?"

Destiny's heart ached with the desire to feel Megan's lips pressed against hers again. Destiny said with a firm tone in her voice, "Are you sure you want this?"

Megan looked up at her and Destiny looked deep into Megan's eyes and watched as her head slowly nodded.

Destiny held her gaze for a moment longer to be sure and then, without warning, she passionately threw Megan down on the bed.

Megan was stunned as Destiny began pulling off the baggy cotton shorts Megan had put on just before bed and threw them on the ground.

Destiny hastily removed her own clothes and dropped them on the ground as Megan anxiously removed her shirt and bra.

Both of them stark naked now, Destiny kneeled down before the bed and forcefully spread Megan's legs far apart.

Destiny eagerly pushed her face into Megan's waiting pussy.

Megan's body shuddered as Destiny fervently stuck her tongue deep into her and began licking vigorously.

Megan climaxed quickly but Destiny found she could hold Megan there indefinitely as Megan writhed in ecstasy.

Destiny's own pussy was gushing wet and she spared a hand to finger herself into orgasm as Megan began to moan uncontrollably loud.

Eventually, they tired and Destiny pulled back to catch her breath.

They rested for a moment before Destiny looked up at Megan and grinned as she asked, "How did you like that?"

Megan was staring up at the ceiling as she tried to catch her own breath. Then Megan finally said with astonishment, "OH-MY-GOD!"

They both began to laugh as Megan held her hands over her face in amazement. She continued,

"I had no idea it could be… sooo good!"

Destiny knew she meant it. Destiny was no expert on girl-girl sex but she had experimented in college. Nothing like this, of course, but Destiny was sure she knew things that Megan could never have experienced.

Destiny leaned forward again and rested her head on Megan's stomach as Megan's legs spread over her shoulders.

Eventually, Destiny moved up to lie beside Megan's naked body on the bed.

They silently caressed each other, sometimes interlocking fingers and holding hands, as their heavy breathing slowly faded.

The silence in the room was only sporadically interrupted when they would spontaneously begin to giggle like little school girls before eventually going silent again as they continued to touch each other softly.

Destiny heard a distant noise that sounded like the garage door opening. They both turned to look at each other as they strained to listen.

Their eyes grew wide and then suddenly the room was a flurry of activity. They giggled to each other as they hurriedly put their clothes back on and tried to straighten the room up to ensure there were no visible signs of their naughtiness.

They sat on the edge of the bed again and tried to act normal as they waited for Mark to come down the hall and knock on the door to the room, but he never did. Instead, they heard Mark go into his and Destiny's bedroom and close the door behind him.

They both let out a collective sigh of relief. It was late, Destiny noticed, and she turned to Megan smiling and said, "We'll talk later. OK?"

Megan smiled back and nodded as Destiny left the room.

Destiny briefly considered telling Mark what had happened, as she knew he would be aroused by it. In fact, she thought, Mark might try and press her to do it again just so he could watch. Destiny wasn't sure how Megan would feel about Mark watching so she ultimately decided not to tell him. Besides, she thought naughtily, *a girl's gotta have some secrets.*

Over the next couple of weeks, Destiny and Megan experimented with each other several times when Mark was away from the house and once while he was just down the hall.

When Mark was home, he usually wouldn't interrupt Destiny and Megan as they talked for hours in Megan's room. One night, while Mark was in the TV room, Destiny and Megan were talking while in Megan's bedroom when things started to get a little too risqué.

Megan seemed to be exceptionally horny that night and she kept trying to seduce Destiny whenever Mark wasn't looking. Mark was watching TV in the other room as Destiny and Megan prepared dinner in the kitchen. Megan kept trying to grope and kiss Destiny as she worked. Destiny acted annoyed each time as she pulled Megan off of her and quietly scolded her to stop it.

Secretly, Destiny enjoyed it when Megan got frisky like this but she was deathly afraid that Mark was going to catch them. Yet the more Destiny rejected Megan's advances, the more horny Megan seemed to become.

At one point, Mark called from the other room, "Aren't you guys done yet? I'm starving." At that same moment, Megan snuck up behind Destiny and began caressing her as she stuck her tongue in Destiny's ear. Destiny had to push her away as she pleaded under her breath, "Stop it! He's going to catch us!" Finally, Destiny replied to Mark out loud, "Just a few more minutes, hon." Megan just smiled back deviously at Destiny's annoyed look.

Just a couple of minutes later, as Destiny was checking the spaghetti, Megan, again, tried to fondle her from behind. Destiny, again, pushed Megan away. Megan frowned and then she grabbed one of Destiny's hands and shoved it down the front of her shorts as she said angrily, "Can't you see how wet I'm getting?" Destiny was a little stunned at how serious Megan had suddenly become. She could tell she was genuinely angry that she wasn't getting what she wanted from Destiny. Destiny pulled her hand out of Megan's shorts. It was covered in Megan's juices. Destiny said, "I'm sorry sweetie but you know we can't do anything when Mark's home."

Megan frowned as she responded, "Yeah, I know. It's just..." Megan didn't finish the statement. Instead she grabbed plates from the cabinet and proceeded to help Destiny serve up dinner without saying anything else.

Throughout dinner, Megan was quite. It was obvious to both Mark and Destiny that Megan was upset but only Destiny knew the reason why. After dinner, Megan talked Destiny into coming into her room so they could talk. Inside her room, Megan seemed to become jubilant again as she resumed her attempts to seduce Destiny. Things got worse from then on.

Destiny repeatedly tried to fend off Megan's advances as she told her, "Stop it!" "No!" "We can't."

Destiny tried to reason with her by explaining that Mark was just down the hall and he might hear them.

Finally, Megan became so frustrated with Destiny's continued rebukes, that she angrily pulled her shorts off, slid back against the headboard, spread her legs wide and began to finger herself right in front of Destiny.

Destiny watched in disbelief as Megan, pouting, stared wantonly into Destiny's eyes. Her face was pleading Destiny to join her as Megan began to finger herself into orgasm.

Destiny was surprised how much Megan reminded her of a spoiled child when she didn't get her way. Destiny wondered, *what kind of monster have I created?*

Unsure of what else to do, Destiny continued to watch helplessly as Megan fingered herself. A moment later, Destiny was starting to get so aroused that she couldn't take it anymore. Eventually, Destiny got up and locked the door. Returning to the bed, Destiny whispered, "OK. But we have to be quiet.... Right?"

Megan, excited now that she finally got her way, nodded eagerly as she continued to finger herself. Destiny quickly removed her shorts and panties in one motion but left her bra and shirt on as she crawled up into bed between Megan's spread legs.

Then Destiny went down on Megan.

Megan tried to control her moaning and gasps of pleasure as Destiny brought her quickly to climax and held her there.

Destiny blindly reached around for a pillow and grasping one, she pushed it toward Megan.

Destiny paused long enough to instruct, "Here. Hold this over your mouth."

Without responding, Megan did as instructed and Destiny went back down on her.

Over the next half hour, Megan's body intermittently convulsed and quivered as she tried to smother her gasps and moans with the pillow.

As Destiny listened to Megan's muted sounds, she fingered herself into orgasm with her free hand.

Eventually, they tired.

Destiny rested for a moment with her head between Megan's thighs as her hands gently caressed Megan's sides. Destiny knew this sometimes drove Megan wild.

The room was quite now and Destiny could hear the distant sound of the TV playing down the hall from them.

Eventually, Destiny asked softly, "Better now?"

Megan didn't respond.

Destiny lifted her head up to see a blissful smile on Megan's face; Megan had fallen asleep.

Destiny smiled as she quietly crawled out of bed and put her clothes back on. Destiny tucked Megan in and stealthily exited the room turning off the light as she left.

As Destiny walked down the hall, she smiled as she thought how much she really enjoyed seeing Megan get off while she tongued her. But Destiny was also beginning to realize, *if she doesn't move out soon, eventually Mark is going to catch us.*

Fortunately, the next week Megan had patched things up with Eric and had finally agreed to move back in with him. Destiny was relieved and sad at the same time. Destiny was going to miss having Megan around and she was especially going to miss their "special" times together. But, Megan's presence was also starting to have an impact on her and Mark's relationship. Destiny knew Mark was anxious for their life to get back to normal and so was Destiny.

Mark had also grown used to having Megan around and was a little sad to see her go too. At first, Mark was annoyed at the imposition Megan had imposed on them as it prevented them from continuing their evenings with Ty. Mark had even started to feel cranky since he wasn't getting the kind of sexual gratification he needed.

But recently, Mark had started to have fantasies about Megan; about Megan and Destiny; about him and Megan; and especially about him, Megan and Destiny.

But more powerful than any of these other fantasies Mark had, was the fantasy Mark was starting to have about introducing Megan to Ty. Mark had even started to secretly masturbate as he contemplated ways of arranging a meeting between the two of them and of what might follow if he did. Sometimes as Mark drove home from work late at night, he would imagine that Destiny had secretly invited Ty over to meet Megan this very night and that she and Megan were having a threesome with Ty this very moment. Mark would become so aroused by the idea that he would have to find a private place to park so he could masturbate.

Unfortunately, when he got home, Mark never saw Ty's car in the driveway and he was pretty sure that he never would. He had considered proposing the idea to Destiny of somehow introducing Megan to Ty but he was pretty sure that Destiny had no intention of letting Megan into such a private part of their lives. But now that Megan was moving out, Mark wished he had at least suggested it – just to see if it was a possibility. Now he would never know.

Before Megan left she had one more request of Destiny. Megan had said that she wanted to show Eric she had changed and she wanted to do something special for him. Then she asked Destiny if she would be willing to do it with her in front of Eric. Megan had said, "I just want Eric to watch us play."

Destiny tried to say no, but Megan continued to press her by saying that she could only handle doing this with Destiny right now and if Destiny could do it just this one time, then Megan would feel more comfortable about trying it with a different woman as Eric watched and maybe eventually, allow Eric to join in. Destiny asked, "What about this girl Jessica?"

Megan said that she might be able to do it with Jessica next time but for the first time, she could only see herself doing it with Destiny. Megan begged, "Pleeeez. I would do it for you and Mark."

By now, Megan had become an expert at getting her way with Destiny. She knew Destiny couldn't resist giving in to her when she pouted a certain way and she used this to great affect now as she pleaded with Destiny to do this one last favor for her.

Eventually, Destiny reluctantly caved. She said, "Ok. Just this once."

Destiny thought to herself, *now what have I got myself into?* She knew she couldn't tell Mark what she had agreed to without having to explain how she had gotten into this mess in the first place.

Destiny felt trapped and somehow… obligated to do this. It was, after all, her idea that Megan needed to be more willing to try new things with Eric.

Besides, Destiny thought, she always thought Eric was kind of hot and the thought of him watching as her and Megan did it was kind of arousing and somehow…. familiar.

Megan finally moved out of Mark and Destiny's home that Saturday.

Chapter 8: Helping Others Find Their Way

That next Wednesday, Destiny arrived at Megan and Eric's apartment shortly after 7:00PM. She had already told Mark she would be going over to their house Wednesday to have dinner and hang out with Megan and that she might not be home until late. Which was completely true, she realized.

Still, Destiny was having second thoughts about this. She thought it was bad enough that she had been "experimenting" with Megan while she lived at hers and Mark's house without Mark's knowledge but now, she was about to permit another man to be a part of it when she hadn't allowed Mark to be.

Destiny thought, *am I cheating?* The answer seemed obvious, but was it really? Destiny had reasoned that what she had been doing with Megan in her own home was something that Mark would have approved of if she could have told him about it. But she couldn't have told Mark about it, could she have? Destiny knew that if Mark had found out what Megan and she were up to all those times in the back room, he would have insisted on being allowed to watch them some time and how was she going to convince Megan to allow him to watch? Destiny had even convinced herself that she was actually doing Mark a favor by sparing him from the frustration of not being allowed to be a part of it by not telling him what they had been up to in the first place.-

But now, Destiny wondered if that had all been true. What if Megan would have agreed to let Mark watch? Destiny wondered what would have kept Megan from trying to convince Mark from joining in if she had wanted him to. Destiny doubted that Mark would be able to resist the charms of such a beautiful young woman under those circumstances.

It finally occurred to Destiny that the real reason she had not told Mark was because she didn't want to have to share Mark with

Megan. Yet, Mark was perfectly willing to share her with another man so why wasn't she willing to do the same with him?

Destiny began to realize just how fortunate she was to be with such a loving and unselfish man such as Mark and she wondered if she would ever be able to unselfishly share him with another woman as he had shared her with another man. Destiny thought, *someday perhaps I will.*

Her thoughts turned back to the present situation as she asked herself, w*hat am I doing here?* And the answer was simple: because Destiny had kept her affair with Megan a secret from Mark, she was now unable to tell Mark what Megan had requested (demanded?) of her and why, without having to confess about the affair her and Megan had been having. Destiny suspected that Mark would have given her permission to do a private girl-on-girl show for Eric if it meant saving the couple's marriage. *If only she would had have told him about her and Megan in the first place,* she thought.

Destiny decided that she would never again keep secrets from Mark. Well, at least not the existence of an entire affair (even if it was only with another woman). But for now, Destiny thought, *let's just get this over with.*

Destiny stepped out of her car and went into Megan and Eric's apartment.

Inside, Destiny sensed some tension in the air and she noticed that Eric seemed to be smiling at her a lot. Obviously, Megan had already told Eric what she had planned for this evening. They went through two bottles of wine by the time they finished dinner. They moved into the living room and talked for a while until they finished a third bottle. Destiny was feeling a little tipsy by now but at least everybody seemed more relaxed. Destiny was even starting to look forward to this as she sized up Eric. Destiny could see that Eric worked out a lot and she could see his rippling muscles through his tight shirt. Destiny felt herself starting to get aroused.

Throughout their evening, Megan periodically would sneak a kiss in on Destiny while Eric was watching. Presumably, she was trying to get Eric worked up for the main event later. Destiny would reciprocate by pulling her close and holding the kiss a little longer.

Now, as Destiny and Megan sat next to each other on the couch, they began to kiss again. Eric sat across from them in a chair and watched.

Eventually, Megan stood up, grabbed Destiny gently by the hand and led her to their bedroom. Eric followed and closed the door behind them.

Inside, they resumed kissing again as they began to remove each other's clothes. Destiny was surprised to notice that Eric was disrobing, too.

With their clothes completely removed, Megan led Destiny to their bed. Megan lay down on her back and motioned Destiny to lie on top of her straddling one of her legs.

Destiny followed her lead and the two began kissing again as they caressed each other's bodies.

A moment later, Destiny was surprised when she felt another body gently crawl into the bed beside her. Destiny felt a strong hand begin to softly caress her back. Destiny knew this was Eric and she thought to herself, *whatever happened to just watching?*

Destiny was certain Megan wouldn't approve if she found out that Eric had crawled into bed with them and was now touching Destiny. She knew that this whole thing was about to go sideways and she imagined Megan throwing a fit at Eric and stomping out of the house in tears.

Destiny felt a flash of anger at Eric as she thought, *what does he think he is doing? Doesn't he know that this is just going to ruin everything that he and Megan had been working on for the past several weeks!?!*

Destiny was angry. She had worked so hard to get these two back together and now Eric was putting all that into jeopardy just because he couldn't learn to control his libido.

But as angry as Destiny was at Eric, she found herself trying to cover for him as she hid his presence behind her from Megan for as long as possible. Destiny feared that she was only enabling Eric's inappropriate behavior by not saying anything and letting him get away with this but she held out in the hope that Eric would eventually return to his chair undiscovered by Megan and then she could avert a major crisis altogether.

Destiny began to feel Eric's manhood pushing against her backside as he moved even closer to her from behind. Destiny was immediately aroused as she started to feel really naughty for continuing to cover for Eric and allow him to commit these indiscretions without protest. She was even starting to feel complicit in Eric's inappropriate behavior and that somehow really turned her on.

Destiny couldn't help herself as her hand felt around behind her and eventually grasp Eric's cock.

As Destiny began to stroke Eric, she could feel that he was much thicker and longer than Mark.

Destiny surreptitiously looked behind her as Megan's eyes were closed and took a quick glance at Eric's manhood. Eric was bigger than Mark alright, but not quite as big as Ty. Destiny turned her attentions back to Megan before she could notice her being distracted.

Destiny wondered how much longer she and Eric could get away with this and she was amazed that they had not been discovered already. Destiny continued to stroke Eric's cock as he began to finger Destiny from behind.

Destiny expected to be discovered at any moment but she was starting to wonder if she could stroke Eric into ejaculation before

Megan found out and then Eric could return to his chair before Megan could discover otherwise.

Destiny contemplated ways of diffusing the situation if Megan discovered what Destiny was doing to Eric.

Then Destiny was startled to hear Megan whisper into her ear, "I want to watch you and Eric do it for awhile."

Destiny was speechless as she looked into Megan's eyes. Megan was serious, Destiny could tell.

Had Megan changed that much since their first talk about being open to new experiences? Destiny thought to herself.

Before Destiny could respond to her, she felt Megan reaching out underneath her to pull Eric in closer behind Destiny.

Destiny was stunned as she realized, *she new Eric was behind me this whole time!*

Eric wordlessly reached one arm around Destiny and began to message Destiny's breast in full view of Megan.

Megan just smiled mischievously at Destiny as she began to crawl out from underneath her.

Destiny was still in shock as she watched Megan walk over to the chair in the corner of the room and sit down.

Eric was behind Destiny now as he vigorously lifted her up on to her knees so he could mount her from behind.

Destiny was too dumbfounded by what was going on to do anything but comply with Eric's manhandling.

Destiny looked back over to Megan. She had slid down in the chair and had her legs up in the air. Megan was spread eagle and she urgently fingered her pussy with a delicious look on her face as she stared wide-eyed at her and Eric in the bed.

Destiny suddenly felt Eric's cock penetrate her from behind as he mounted her and it caused her to gasp.

Destiny heard Megan moan loudly in response.

Eric held Destiny firmly by the hips as he began to vigorously fuck Destiny.

Destiny grabbed handfuls of the bed sheets as she settled into Eric's forceful rhythm.

Over time, Eric's rhythm grew even stronger and Destiny began to climax.

Destiny was seized by orgasms repeatedly and each time she did, she could hear Megan in the corner chair being seized by her own orgasms in concurrence with hers.

Finally, Destiny felt Eric go rock hard inside her as he began to explode in her pussy.

Destiny waited for Eric to completely finish before she finally collapsed forward onto the bed.

Destiny lay there exhausted trying to catch her breath.

Eric collapsed beside her and Destiny rolled to the side to give him more room.

Destiny felt Megan climb into bed with them. Megan semi-straddled Eric as the two began to kiss and whisper sweet nothings into to each other's ears. After awhile, it seemed to Destiny that the two had fallen into their own little intimate world and were only dimly aware that Destiny was still laying there face down and exhausted beside them.

Eventually, Destiny quietly rolled out of the bed and began to put her clothes on. Megan suddenly aware, pleaded, "Where are you going?"

Destiny smiled at her and answered, "It's late and I have to be getting home sweetie," she added, "Mark's probably waiting up for me."

Megan made a sound of disappointment.

Destiny was contemplative as she tried to make sense out of everything that had happened while she finished getting dressed. Megan got out of the bed to walk her to the door. Eric leaned forward in bed and said sincerely, "Thanks."

Destiny could see that Eric meant it sincerely and was struggling for more to add. Destiny just smiled broadly as she walked over, bent down and kissed him. Destiny said, "It was my pleasure." Destiny turned to the door and then added, "I'm glad to see you two back together again."

Eric then said, "Thanks for helping us… work things out."

Megan gaily leapt pass Destiny in the living room and barred her from reaching the front door. Megan smiling said, "Thanks for everything."

Destiny could see tears begin to well up in Megan's eyes and she began to cry as Megan said, "You saved my marriage."

Destiny began to feel her own tears as she responded, "Ahhh" and gave Megan a long hug.

Finally, the two released each other and Destiny exited the apartment.

On the drive home, Destiny contemplated everything that had happened that night and slowly it began to sink into Destiny's conscious that Megan had become a 'Watcher'.

Destiny suspected that it had something to do with the day that she had walked in on Eric and that stranger fucking Jessica. Destiny thought that this may have had more of an impact on Megan than

Destiny had realized. Megan was very upset that day but Destiny wondered if she was conflicted about what she saw because she was probably also extremely aroused at seeing Eric with another woman.

Destiny wondered if Megan had always been a watcher but it had taken her walking in on Eric with another woman before she could discover that about herself.

Destiny smiled to herself as she thought how everything had come full circle for Megan. Destiny considered, at first Megan couldn't deal with Eric's sexual fantasy for a threesome; she even suspected that Eric was just using it as a way to sleep with her friends, now Megan actually got off on watching Eric have sex with another woman. *How much things had changed,* Destiny thought to herself.

Destiny suspected that Megan and Eric would have a long and happy marriage.

Destiny desperately wanted to share her story with Mark and she decided when she got home, she would find a way to tell him…. Everything.

Mark felt a little disappointed in Destiny as she shared the events of the past few weeks. Mostly, he was disappointed that she had been withholding so much from him.

When she got to the part about Megan asking her to do it with her while Eric watched and she agreed without consulting with Mark first, he admittedly felt a little betrayed. Destiny explained to Mark how she had felt trapped by her previous deceptions and how that prevented her from consulting with Mark about Megan's proposition.

Mark ultimately agreed with Destiny's intuition that he would have probably been OK with her having a threesome with them had Mark known about everything else that was going on in the first place.

Then Destiny told Mark how the plans had somehow changed once she was in their bedroom making-out with Megan. Destiny told Mark how Eric had snuck into bed behind Destiny, how Destiny found herself stroking Eric's cock as she tried to hide it from Megan and how she found out that Megan knew Eric was behind Destiny touching her all along.

Destiny confessed to Mark how she had somehow been bamboozled when Megan unexpectedly got out of bed and went over to the chair to play with herself while she left Eric to have his way with Destiny for the rest of the evening.

Destiny said, "If I had known that was what she really had in mind, I would have definitely declined Megan's proposition…. At least until I found a way to talk to you first."

Mark believed her. He realized that her honesty with him was much more important to him than who she had actually had sex with. Mark found he was only disappointed with her for not telling him what she was up to beforehand.

Destiny promised Mark she would never keep such things secret from him again.

Chapter 9: Getting Reacquainted With Old Friends

Over the next few weeks, things gradually began to return to normal again. Mark and Destiny felt they needed a break after all the craziness they had been through to focus more on their own relationship.

It was a Saturday morning when Destiny, folding a load of laundry, found herself reminiscing about the adventures they had with Ty. She had felt bad that they had not contacted him since their last night together. Destiny tried to calculate when that had been and was surprised to find it had been at least four months or more since they had last spoken with Ty. Destiny wondered if Ty was still around and if he was, would he even still be interested in seeing them again? She thought they should have at least called him at some point to let him know they were still thinking about him.

Destiny decided that she would give Ty a call just to let him know that they had not forgotten about him and maybe, just maybe, if Ty wasn't doing anything tonight...and Mark was interested, maybe they could get together tonight. Destiny's body shuddered and she suddenly grew wet as she considered the possibility of being ravaged by Ty in just a few hours from now.

Destiny approached Mark, who had been working on something in the garage, and asked, "Honey? How would you feel about seeing Ty tonight? Or sometime soon?"

Mark had been thinking a lot about Ty and Destiny lately and although he really wanted to see the two of them together again, he could not seem to find a good time to bring the subject up with Destiny. It seemed to Mark that so much time had passed since their last encounter with Ty, and then the drama with Megan's marriage, that Destiny seemed to not be interested in their adventures with black men anymore… Or at least, not interested for the moment.

Mark was pleased now to hear that Destiny was thinking about being taken by a black man again and he was glad that she was the one making the suggestion to call Ty. Mark tried to contain his enthusiasm as he responded, "Yeah, sure, if you want to," and then not feeling it sounded enthusiastic enough for her added, "I mean, if you want to, I would like that… a lot."

Destiny smiled as she could see Mark was very excited about the idea even though he tried to pretend it wasn't that big of a deal to him. Destiny said, "Let's try calling him then."

The matter being settled, Mark dropped what he was doing and they went to their office to make the call.

Destiny was pleasantly surprised to hear his deep voice again as he answered, "Hello Destiny… Long time no hear."

Destiny said hello and began her apologies for not calling him in so long. Destiny explained the reasons why. Ty seemed unaffected by their long absence. Eventually, Destiny got around to asking Ty if he was free and willing to get together tonight and Ty responded he already had plans for the evening but after a moment of hesitation, he said that he might be able to get out of them but that he would need to make some calls first. Ty asked, "Can I call you back in an hour?" Destiny answered, "Sure," before adding, "Wait, do you still have our home number?"

Ty said, "Maybe…But you better give it to me again anyway."

She gave Ty their home number then they hung up.

Destiny went back to doing her chores as she waited with deep anticipation for Ty to call them back. It was 11:30AM now and their phone rang at 12:15PM.

Destiny answered, "Hello?"

Ty answered, "Hi, Destiny."

Destiny replied, "Hi, Ty"

Ty began, "Well it looks like I can make it tonight after all."

Destiny's heart raced with excitement and she had to take a moment to calm herself before she could respond.

Destiny said, "That's Great." She paused for a moment before asking, "Is eight-o-clock OK for you?"

Ty answered, "That sounds fine."

A moment of uncomfortable silence passed before Destiny said, "OK, then eight-o-clock it is."

Ty responded, "See you then." And they hung up.

As the day wore on, both Mark and Destiny began to feel their anticipation for the evening build. It had been some time since their last encounter and they were now feeling butterflies in their stomachs as they felt some apprehension about meeting Ty after so much time had gone by. In a way they felt that it seemed like meeting Ty again for the first time. *What would they talk about?* they each wondered.

As they got ready for the evening, Mark and Destiny expected the night to play out somewhat like the last time Ty came over.

Tonight, Destiny decided to wear a red pleather miniskirt with white stockings and red high heels. She opted to wear her new white lace corset she had bought a couple of weeks ago underneath her blouse.

Ty arrived just after 8:00PM. Mark answered the door and said, "Hey Ty, come on in."

Destiny came out of the bedroom to greet Ty.

"Hello," Destiny said with a smile.

She imagined throwing her arms around Ty and kissing as they usually did but found herself hesitating instead. Destiny realized that so much time had passed since their last encounter that she was suddenly feeling a little awkward and uncomfortable at meeting Ty again. Destiny was unsure what level of formality the occasion called for.

Unsure of how she should proceed, Destiny found herself reaching out with her hand to shake Ty's. Ty reached out and held her hand and kissed it as he said, "You look ravishing… as always."

Destiny felt a tingling sensation flow up through her arm and then unexpectedly, she found herself embracing Ty as the two kissed albeit just a short one.

Mark was feeling a little awkward himself. He asked, "What are you having?"

"A beer is fine," responded Ty.

Destiny and Ty went into the living room as Mark went to get drinks from the kitchen. When Mark returned, Destiny was showing Ty some pictures hanging on the wall from their vacation to a Sandals Resort in the Caribbean last year.

Mark handed Ty his beer and Destiny a glass of wine. It occurred to Destiny that Ty had never really seen their home before and she found herself giving him a tour. Destiny thought, *this isn't how I expected the evening to start.*

Destiny took another drink from her glass of wine hoping that it would help to loosen her up a little bit as she tried to think of ways to bring their conversation around to something more intimate and erotic.

As she was showing Ty the backyard, Ty said, "So, you guys have a hot tub," with a slight grin on his face.

Their hot tub sat on top of a deck overlooking the city lights below. There was a three-sided gazebo of sorts to shelter the hot tub from the wind as well as on-looking neighbors. Destiny replied, "Yeah, we do," and as she started to understand what Ty was getting at, she added, "We should try it some time," as she grinned naughtily back at Ty.

"Why not now?" said Ty with a hint of enthusiasm.

Destiny and Mark, shocked, looked at each other for a moment and simultaneously they could not come up with any reason why now would be a bad time. It wasn't what they expected to happen with tonight's encounter but they had discovered things rarely turned out the way you expect them to with these types of things.

"You want to?" Destiny said as she stared at Mark.

"Sounds fine to me," Mark offered indifferently.

Destiny said a little excitedly, "OK. Well, I'll need to change and... what is Ty going to wear?" as she began to work out the details.

Mark offered, "I'm sure I have a pair of shorts he could wear."

Destiny looked at Ty's frame and then back to Mark's and said skeptically, "Maybe."

Destiny went off to the bedroom to check as Mark and Ty tried to make conversation. She returned shortly wearing a shiny black two-piece French cut bikini with a wrap. She carried an old pair of Mark's shorts.

"Try these on," she said to Ty and handed them to him.

Ty grinned as he accepted the shorts and then hesitantly, he headed towards the back bathroom to put them on as Mark headed to their bedroom to change also.

They returned to the kitchen to find Destiny holding a stack of towels.

"Ready?" she said cheerfully.

They grabbed their drinks and headed outside.

The night air was cool and dry with only the slightest breeze. A sliver of the moon showed on the horizon. They whispered quietly to each other as Mark and Ty removed the protective top and began to climb in.

Mark and Ty watched as Destiny removed her wrap and began climbing into the hot tub with them and as she did, Mark noticed how fit and toned her body had become over the past several months. Mark couldn't remember a time where she had looked even hotter than she did now. As everybody slowly worked into the hot water, Mark turned on the jets.

They sat in their individual seats quietly getting acquainted with the different jets that were available. It was a square hot tub and Ty chose the master seat, which was a contoured seat prominently located in the center of one of the sides and was slightly reclined as it protruded towards the middle of the hot tub.

Mark and Destiny sat opposite each other on the sides to the left and right of Ty. No one spoke for a couple of minutes as they enjoyed the massaging action of the jets and sipped their drinks.

Mark and Destiny were contemplating ways of breaking the ice when finally Ty looked over at Destiny as she sipped on her wine and said matter-of-factly, "Why don't you take your bikini off?"

Destiny choked on her drink at the unexpected bluntness of Ty's suggestion. Yet, inexplicably, Destiny's first reaction to Ty's suggestion was to feel offended at the presumptuous nature of it and that as a woman she was somehow obligated to defend her honor.

Destiny chuckled in disbelief for a moment as she searched for an appropriate response. Unsure of how she should respond, Destiny looked over to Mark to gauge his reaction and to get an indication of how maybe she should be reacting.

Mark returned a grin that said 'just go with it'.

Finally, Destiny replied simply, "OK," with an almost reluctant tone of resignation in her voice.

Mark and Ty watched as Destiny stood up and removed her bottom piece.

Destiny was feeling a little self-conscious as they watched. She couldn't understand why she was having such a hard time letting go of her inhibitions this time.

Ty removed his shorts and put them on the edge of the hot tub before he rose slowly out of his seat to stand closely behind Destiny.

Ty gently put his hands on her hips; slowly he pulled her closer and began to kiss Destiny's neck from behind.

Destiny's eyes opened wide for a moment as she felt his thick stiff rod grinding against her lower back.

Ty's hand came up under her arms to massage both her breasts. Destiny's eyes closed as she finally began to lose herself in Ty's caressing hands.

Eventually, Ty began to guide her backwards toward his seat.

Destiny wasn't sure what Ty was trying to do so she asked, "Where are we going?"

Ty didn't bother to respond. Instead, Destiny began to realize that Ty was motioning her to sit on his lap so he could feed his massive cock up inside of her as she rested there.

Destiny hadn't played with any of her dildos in months and wasn't sure if she could still take something as large as Ty's cock inside her without some practice first.

Unsure of herself, she pleaded, "I don't know if I can do this yet."

Ty responded in a reassuring tone, "Don't worry, we'll go slow."

Comforted by Ty's words, Destiny proceeded to spread her feet a little as she adjusted her position in front of Ty.

Ty continued to hold her by her hips as she put one hand between her legs into the water to feel for Ty's rod.

She found it and grabbed a hold as she began to bend her legs seeking contact with the head of Ty's cock and her pussy.

Her eyes widened as it made contact.

She took a deep breath and let it out as she began to work it into her.

Her eyes closed and she clenched her teeth as she felt his enormous head spreading her lips as it pushed inside her.

Mark was already holding his throbbing penis in his hand as he sat there motionless and at full attention.

He was fixated on the scene of his wife impaling herself on her black stud's enormous cock.

Mark watched as Destiny lowered herself deeper on to Ty's massive cock and Ty continued to guide her down with his hands on her hips.

Destiny's back was arched and her head was tilted up to the starry night as she slowly exhaled through her mouth.

Her eyes were closed as she sank lower into the water and deeper onto Ty.

Destiny had to occasionally pause her descent in order to get used to Ty's massive cock inside her. She thought, *it's been so long – Too long.*

Looking down at the small of Destiny's back, Ty said softly and reassuringly, "You're almost there."

Destiny broke out into laughter, disturbing the silence of the night, as she replied sarcastically, "Yeah, right."

Destiny could tell Ty's cock was only a little bit over half way inside her. She still had a good four inches to go before she would be resting on his lap.

Destiny, determined, took another deep breath and began descending further down on Ty's cock with a subtle look of pain forming on her face.

Eventually, after what seemed like several minutes, Destiny found herself resting on Ty's lap.

His cock was so deep inside that she had to be very careful with her movements. Any sudden movements she made would cause a shock of pain to shoot up through her.

Ty instructed softly, "Alright, now have a sip of your wine and lean back."

Destiny, still breathing through her mouth in short gasps, opened her eyes and motioned towards Mark to hand her the glass of wine which was still sitting on the edge of the hot tub just out of her reach.

Mark rose up, moved to the other side, fetched the glass and put it in her outstretched hand.

Destiny took a deep gulp from the glass and moved it down below her face.

Ty said encouragingly, "Good. Now lean back."

Destiny gasped as she began to lean back and Ty quickly added, "Slowly!"

Destiny continued to slowly lean back towards Ty's chest.

Ty said softly, "That's good. Now just rest there for awhile."

Destiny, in immense pain/pleasure, softly squeaked out, "OK."

After a moment, Ty turned to Mark and said in a startlingly casual voice, "Now tell me more about this Sandals place."

Mark suddenly shaken from his wide-eyed trance, stopped stroking himself and searched for words as he tried to regain his composure.

Mark began to tell Ty about the Sandals resort they visited. All the while, Destiny quietly sat there in Ty's lap facing forward with her eyes closed, her glass held out in front of her.

She seemed very distant from the conversation. She slowly breathed in and out of her mouth while she got acclimated to her current condition of having ten inches of hard black cock shoved deep inside her.

Mark was impressed at the level of control Ty exerted over the situation. He thought, *here is this big black guy with his enormous cock shoved deep inside my wife's pussy and he is still able to sit there and engage in a casual conversation with me about some resort we visited like it's no big deal.*

Mark sat there deeply admiring Ty's masculinity.

Mark occasionally had trouble concentrating on the conversation, as Ty, not seeming to be distracted at all, continued to ask a variety of questions about Sandals. After several minutes of the exchange, Mark was answering one of Ty's questions when he was suddenly aware of the look on Destiny's face.

Her expression had not changed for some time now. She continued to face forward with her eyes closed and her glass held up in her hand.

Her breathing was slow and shallow but he could now hear an occasional, soft and barely audible whimper coming from her mouth.

Mark stopped in mid-sentence and said in a concerned voice, "Destiny?"

Destiny's eyes remained closed as she responded meekly with a slight tremor in her voice, "Uh huh."

Mark asked, "Are you alright?"

Destiny responded again, "Uh huh."

Ty grinned at her response.

Mark explained, "You look like you're ready to pass out."

Destiny replied again with an identical, "Uh huh."

Both Mark and Ty chuckled at her responses.

Then it suddenly came to Mark, that soft whimper - Destiny was actually in the throes of an orgasm.

It occurred to Mark, that the whole time he and Ty discussed Sandals, Destiny was sitting there on Ty's cock having a long, continuous string of subtle orgasms as she had sometimes done on the dildos she occasionally played with.

Suddenly aware of what was happening and not wanting to distract her, Mark went back to answering Ty's questions about

Sandals trying not to be distracted himself by the occasional whimpers still coming from Destiny's mouth.

Mark talked with Ty but was mindful of the fact that she could pass out at anytime. He stood at the ready to catch her if she did.

Twenty minutes later, Mark noticed as Destiny began to re-open her eyes and come back from the distant place she had been.

She was blankly staring outward towards the city lights, occasionally taking a drink from her glass and still lost in her thoughts.

Ty and Mark were still taking about resorts when Destiny began to tune into the conversation and eventually she even began to join in.

As the three talked, it occurred to Mark a number of times just-how surreal this situation had become. *Here we were, having a casual conversation on different resorts while Ty's cock was shoved all the way up into Destiny's pussy.* The situation was made real by the occasional gasps Destiny made in the middle of the discussion when Ty sometimes repositioned himself in the seat.

To Mark, this reaction by Destiny reaffirmed the fact that Ty was still very hard and inserted completely inside of Destiny.

They continued the discussion until Mark noticed both Ty's beer and Destiny's glass were empty. Mark looked at his and saw it was still full. Mark offered to go inside and get Ty another beer and fill up Destiny's glass.

As Mark entered the back door, he looked over his shoulder at the two. Destiny was still sitting on Ty's lap and their backs were to him. He could see Ty saying something into her ear and Destiny responded with a laugh followed by a sudden gasp and then another laugh. Mark smiled to himself, *still rock hard inside her,* as he closed the door behind him.

Inside, Mark looked in the fridge and realized he had to go to the downstairs bar fridge for Ty's beer. When he returned to the kitchen, Mark quickly checked up on them through the kitchen window and decided to go to the bathroom while he had the chance.

Mark had difficulty peeing, as his penis was still hard. Looking down at it, Mark couldn't help but to think how small his was compared to Ty's. He couldn't see Ty's cock in the hot tub because it was below water. But he was well aware of how enormous Ty's cock was from their previous encounters. Lost in those thoughts for a moment, Mark flushed the toilet and returned to the kitchen.

Mark refilled Destiny's glass of wine. As he was heading back to the hot tub, Mark thought he could see Destiny's body moving up and down on Ty's lap. Mark wasn't sure at first if she was really moving because the movement was very subtle. As Mark arrived at the hot tub standing in front of them, he suddenly became aware that they were in the middle of something and he was interrupting them.

They both turned their heads to look at Mark. Destiny continued to move rhythmically on Ty's lap as she stared blankly into Mark's eyes. It was clear to Mark that Destiny was lost in pleasure and incapable of speaking for the moment. Instead, Destiny let Ty speak for her. Ty suggested, "Why don't you give us a little more time?"

Almost without hesitation, Mark said apologetically, "Yeah, sure, no problem," and immediately did an about-face, drinks still in his hand, and headed back towards the house, closing the door behind him.

Inside, Mark decided to mix himself a new drink as he thought about how readily he obeyed Ty's request. Mark also felt aroused by the fact that Destiny didn't say a word to counter Ty's suggestion. Mark thought, *clearly, she realized that Ty was the one in charge*. Mark found himself extremely turned on by the new roles that were being handed out by Ty during their encounters.

Curious as to what they were doing right now, Mark made his way from the kitchen to the back door. Mark slowly and quietly opened the back door. As he quietly moved outside, he began to hear them. Destiny was still moving up and down rhythmically on Ty's lap and she let out a moan on every stroke. Ty was also making sounds. Mark could now hear him say, "Uh Huh, that's my girl," followed by, "You like that. Don't you?"

To which Destiny would always reply in a moaning voice, "Uh Huh."

Mark walked up a little closer confident they couldn't see him as the backyard was dark and both their backs were to him. Mark thought he could hear Ty say, "Who's your Big Daddy now?"

To which Destiny replied enthusiastically, "You Are!" and Mark saw the intensity of Destiny's rhythm and moaning increase sharply.

Destiny continued her up and down motion on Ty as Mark watched her motions began to get more furious. Clearly, she was working Ty up into an orgasm as well as herself. Not wanting to risk being discovered and ruining the moment, Mark tiptoed back to the house and went inside.

Mark went to the leaving room and sat down on the couch. His heart was racing and his cock was rock hard. He shoved his hand down his swim trunks and began stroking his penis fast and hard. He decided to remove his shorts as they were getting in the way of his stroking.

Mark sat there stroking his small white penis as hard and fast as he could as he thought about the situation his wife was in right now outside. Mark thought, *Ty was about to explode in his wife's pussy and he wasn't doing anything about it. He may even be coming inside her right now.* Mark wondered what it must feel like to have Ty's enormous black cock shoved deep inside.

This thought made Mark explode as white cum shot out of his penis landing all over his legs and groin. Mark sat there for a few minutes while he savored the ecstasy of his orgasm and tried to catch his breath.

Eventually, Mark realized that he had been gone for a quite a long time. Mark cleaned up quickly and put his shorts back on. He looked out the window to see what Ty and Destiny were doing now. As he suspected, the motion had stopped and the two appeared to be reclining back. Ty's face was to the stars and it appeared Destiny was lying back on his chest.

Mark quickly grabbed the drinks and made his way back to the hot tub. He found them there, Destiny leaning back, resting her head on his chest. Both of them were looking up into the night sky. They were both breathing hard when they turned their heads momentarily to see Mark arriving back at the hot tub and smiled at him. Neither of them said anything as Mark climb back into the hot tub. They were still trying to catch their breaths, Mark could see. Mark handed Ty his beer and Destiny her glass of wine.

After awhile, Mark, trying to break the silence, mentioned how great the weather was tonight. Destiny and Ty agreed. As they began to talk, Destiny eventually said, "OK, I need to get up now," and proceeded to lean forward and slowly stand up removing Ty's cock from her pussy. She moved over to the side and sat down.

The three of them continued to talk about a number of mundane things for another hour as they consumed their drinks.

Eventually, Destiny said, "I'm getting water logged," as she looked at her hands. "Should we go inside now?" she asked.

Everybody agreed.

They dried off and went inside,-changed back into their original clothes and had some more drinks as they talked in the living room.

Destiny sat on the couch snugly leaning into Ty's chest with his arm around her shoulders as she sipped her wine. Mark sat opposite of them in a leather chair. Mark thought amusedly, *if a stranger came upon them right now, it would appear that Destiny and Ty were the married couple and Mark was just some mutual friend.*

Mark imagined for a moment the three of them sitting in an anonymous lounge somewhere with Ty's arm around Destiny just like he had right now and he strangely found the thought arousing.

Mark somehow liked the idea of strangers seeing Destiny in the arms of a strong black man, of strangers knowing that she got thoroughly fucked every night by his massive black cock.

Mark wondered if maybe they should invite Ty on their next vacation. Mark would then propose that in public, they should pretend to be a couple and he would just pretend to be a friend and no one would be the wiser. Mark found this crazy idea very arousing.

Eventually, Mark noticed Destiny moving her hand over Ty's groin and gently rub Ty's cock through his pants as they causally talked. Mark looked on as the bulge in his pants grew.

The three continued talking for awhile. Occasionally, while Mark carried the conversation along, Destiny would look up into Ty's face; they would smile at each other and then would softly kiss before returning to the conversation.

After awhile, when things got quiet, Destiny looked up at Ty and asked, "Should we retire to the bedroom?"

Ty smiled at her and began to stand up. As the two walked towards the bedroom holding hands, Mark was unsure if he was supposed to go with them or stay here. Ty hadn't suggested either way and even Mark was unsure of what he wanted to do.

Normally, Mark had accompanied them and watched as Destiny was taken by Ty. But tonight, Mark found it equally exciting to stay out of the room and let Ty and Destiny enjoy a little private time as Mark stroked his penis alone in the living room.

Still unsure, Mark decided he would wait a few minutes to let them at least get started before he decided if he wanted to join in or not.

They left the door open and Mark strained to hear from the living room as he imagined what they were doing inside the bedroom. Mark could hear sounds that made his heart flutter as he began to put the sounds into context.

Eventually, Mark saw someone close the door. He was not sure if it was Ty or Destiny who had closed it but he found the thought arousing either way.

Mark leaned back in the living room chair as he slowly stroked his penis. He became lost in his thoughts as he fell into a deep ecstasy and when he began to hear Destiny loudly moaning in the other room, he came all over himself endlessly. Mark grinned at the pleasure and eventually fell asleep with cum spread all over his lap.

Later he woke and saw the bedroom door still closed. Mark wasn't sure what time it was but he was extremely tired as he made his way down the hall to the guest bedroom and fell back to sleep.

Sometime later, Mark was disturbed from his sleep as Destiny gently shook him awake. Destiny stood in a robe before him as he dimly became aware that it was starting to get light outside and he looked over to the clock on the wall. It was 6:30AM. Destiny softly said, "It's time to come to bed," and began leading him to their bedroom.

Mark asked confused and sleepily, "Where's Ty?"

Destiny replied softly, "He just left. Come to bed."

As she said this, Mark noticed the calm satisfied look in her face and words. He thought how beautiful she was, especially lately, as the two laid down in bed and fell asleep together.

Later that morning, Mark awoke and took a shower. He left the bedroom quietly and closed the door behind him as Destiny was still sleeping. Mark began his morning routine.

Chapter 10: More Friends

By Wednesday, Mark was unable to get the events of last Saturday out of his mind. He tried to remember what time it was when Destiny and Ty left for the bedroom. He guessed it was probably around nine-thirty or ten. He thought, *they had spent the entire rest of the night together in our bedroom,* as he tried to imagine all the sexual acts they must have performed while he slept in the guest bedroom.

Mark wanted more and he didn't want to wait until the weekend. Mark decided to ask Destiny when he got home from work if she would be interested in meeting Ty again tonight and hoped he would be available if she said yes.

Mark was glad to find that Destiny was interested in another encounter with Ty that evening and they decided to call Ty to see if he was available.

Ty answered the phone with his now usual charming, "Hello Destiny."

Destiny responded with her now usual, "Hello Ty," in the same inflection as Ty.

She continued, "What are you up to?"

Ty replied, "Oh, just hangin' out with a couple of my old college friends." He continued, "They are from out of town and are staying with me for a couple of days."

Destiny said, "Well. That sounds like a lot of fun."

Ty continued, "Yeah, they made me take them to a couple of singles bars last night so we are just kicking back tonight."

Destiny began to suspect that Ty would not be available tonight. Destiny said, "Oh. Well I hope you guys had fun."

Ty replied, "Oh yeah. We had fun alright."

A moment of silence passed before Destiny began, "Well...We were just wondering if you would be interested at all in coming over tonight?" with a level of hopefulness in her voice.

Ty responded contemplatively, "Hmmm. I would like to but I don't know if I could leave these clowns alone for that long."

Ty paused for a moment and then continued doubtfully, "Well. Let me see what I could do... Can I call you back in a few?"

Destiny replied cheerfully, "Sure. No problem,"

They both hung up.

Mark and Destiny waited hopefully for Ty to call back. Twenty minutes later the phone rang and Destiny answered, seeing it was Ty.

"Hi Ty", she said in a naughty voice.

Ty replied the same, "Hi Destiny."

Destiny began hopefully, "So... are we going to see you tonight?"

Ty answered, "Well. I got a little bit of a problem..." and continued, "I had to explain to my friends about are... arrangement. And now they insist on coming with me."

Destiny broke into laughter and Mark, listening to the conversation, broke into laughter too.

Finally, Destiny said amusedly, "Oh they do, do they?"

Destiny was feeling a little aroused now at the idea that there were two other men, whom she didn't even know, that were lusting after her right now.

Ty began to explain, "Yeah they..." and Mark and Destiny could hear other voices in the background now.

Ty interrupted himself and said, "One of them really wants to talk to you."

Destiny replied, "Well put him on then."

After a moment, Destiny heard another voice come on the phone.

"Hi Destiny", the charming deep voice said.

Destiny said in a naughty voice, "Well hello there. Who's this?"

He replied, "This is Sean...Hey I saw a picture of you."

Destiny remembered the picture they had sent Ty through AFF a long time ago and began to feel extremely naughty knowing that this stranger had seen a picture of her posing in a slutty dress.

Destiny said, "Oh really. And what do you think?"

Mark was feeling really turned on listening to Destiny flirt with this stranger.

After a moment, Sean said, "I think you are one hot woman and I think you should let John and I accompany Ty over to your house tonight for a little fun."

Destiny was speechless for a moment as she began to feel herself getting really turned on by the idea. She looked into Mark's eyes as she began to respond. The words seem to fall uncontrollably out of her mouth as she said in a dirty voice, "Well, maybe I'll let you."

Mark's eyes went wide for a moment as he considered what Destiny was suggesting. Mark imagined for a moment Destiny getting gang-banged by three huge black studs and found himself incredibly aroused at the thought.

Finally, unable to contain his desire, Mark whispered to Destiny enthusiastically, "Yes...let's do it...invite them over."

Mark knew that he should be exercising more caution since they didn't really know anything about Ty's friends. *What if they got out of control and started hurting Destiny? Could he stop them?* Mark knew this situation could become dangerous really quick but he couldn't help himself. He was lost in his desire to see Destiny getting gang-banged and he couldn't think of anything else.

Sean asked enthusiastically, "How soon do you want us there?"

Destiny, starting to have second thoughts about what she was really getting herself into, answered, "I don't know....ummm...Let me talk to Ty again. OK?"

Ty came back on the phone and said to Destiny somewhat apologetically, "You know, you don't have to do this. I could come over by myself if you really want."

Destiny replied, "Hmmm," as she carefully considered what she wanted.

Ty continued encouragingly, "But I think you would like them."

Destiny remained quiet as she was a little concerned she was getting in over her head. On one hand the idea of being 'taken' by three black men was very arousing to her but on the other hand, she wasn't quite sure she could handle three men at once. At least, not yet. *Could she?* Destiny wished she could have more time to work up to something like this but she realized that this could be a one-time opportunity and she didn't want to pass it up. Destiny thought, *what if they get too rough? Mark wouldn't be able to stop them for sure.* Destiny felt herself getting even more aroused at the thought of having no control over the situation if it got out of hand. She truly would be at their mercy.

A long moment of silence had passed as Destiny considered everything. She could tell that everyone was waiting intently for her to respond. Finally, unable to admit out loud that she really wanted to be gang-banged, Destiny replied ambiguously, "Does eight-o-clock work for you?"

Ty calmly answered, "eight-o-clock is fine."

Destiny finished the call by saying, "OK. We'll see you then."

Mark wondered for a moment if Destiny understood that Ty was going to bring his friends with him tonight and that they weren't coming over just for drinks. Mark said matter-of-factly, "So, he is bringing his friends over."

Destiny didn't look at Mark as she began to organize her desk and said smugly, "Uh. Huh."

Mark then asked in a concerned voice, "Are you sure you're OK with this?"

Destiny answered as if it was no big deal, "Sure. Aren't you?"

Mark replied, "Definitely."

Mark now knew Destiny understood what this meant and he was stunned at the idea that his wife, who was normally very shy and reserved, was ready to be gang-banged. Mark was very turned on by this new ultra-sexual wife of his.

Destiny decided to wear the same ensemble she wore the first time Ty came over.

The doorbell rang just before eight. Mark opened the door and found three gentlemen standing there. Mark said, "Hey. How's it goin'?" and motioned them in.

Ty walked through the door first. Destiny, who was standing behind Mark, smiled and moved in to embrace Ty. They gently embraced each other and then, looking up into his eyes, she said, "Hi Ty," and proceeded to kiss him softly.

Destiny then released Ty as he moved further into the room to make room for his two friends to file in through the door.

Destiny looked up at another black gentleman who was standing before her. Destiny noted that he was even taller than Ty and very handsome. Smiling, he said in a deep voice, "Hi. I'm John."

Destiny responded seductively, "Hi John," as she offered him a hug and he accepted it.

Mark couldn't help but notice with some awe just how tiny Destiny looked while she held John's embrace.

John moved out of the way as the last gentlemen filed in.

Now standing before Destiny was a black man with very broad shoulders. She noted that this one worked out a lot. He had muscles that rippled all over his body. He wasn't as tall as the other two but he was still very handsome. He said smiling, "Hi Destiny. I'm Sean. Can I get a kiss like Ty?"

Destiny immediately recognized Sean as the clown of the three.

Destiny smiled and said, "Hi Sean and yes, you certainly can," as she leaned forward and kissed him.

A moment of awkward silence passed before Mark said, "Can I get you guys something to drink?" Ty said, "Beer would be fine, if you have any?"

Mark said, "I'm sure we do," as he headed towards the kitchen.

Destiny said, "Have a seat," as she motioned them towards the living room.

As they moved into the living room, Sean said, "I really like your dress."

Destiny replied smiling, "Why thank you," as she sat down on the couch. Sean and John sat in the chairs to each side of her and Ty sat in the chair directly across from her.

Destiny was feeling a little nervous now being surrounded by three strong black men and she did her best to hide it.

Sean said, "I like your shoes, too," as he got up again and moved over to the couch to sit next to her.

Destiny replied, "Thank you," and before she knew it, John also moved to the couch and sat next to her on the other side.

John asked, "Where did you get the dress?"

Destiny answered, "Actually, I bought it online..." and before she could finish, Sean asked, "What is it made of?"

Destiny, interrupted, answered "Pleather," as Sean began to touch her dress.

John said, "It is very sexy."

Destiny responded, "Thank you. I'm glad you like it."

Destiny was beginning to feel a little overwhelmed as John began feeling her dress, too. She thought, *they're like a pack of wolves circling their prey and I'm the prey!* Destiny fought to control the incredible sense of arousal she was feeling as these two men accosted her and fought for her attention.

Sean said, "You have real pretty eyes."

Destiny replied, "Thanks," and offered in return, "You work out a lot, don't you?"

Sean answered smugly, "Two hours a day."

Mark returned from the kitchen with three beers and put two on the coffee table for Sean and John and handed the third to Ty.

Ty absently took the beer as he watched the barrage of questions Sean and John were asking Destiny.

Mark thought, *Wow! This is progressing quickly.*

Mark returned to the kitchen to grab his drink. When he returned, he stood next to Ty.

Mark could see Sean and John exploring Destiny's clothes and they seemed to be full of questions. Destiny was trying to keep up with all the questions. Her face was blushing a deep red and she looked so young and innocent as she was crowded and touched by these two large black men, Mark thought.

Ty, with a concerned look on his face, was intently watching the three on the couch.

Mark, looking for something to break the silence with Ty said, "So. How have you been?"

Ty ignored Mark's question, as his mind seemed to be occupied with other thoughts. Instead, Ty stood up and turned to Mark as he said quietly and with a serious voice, "I think you should lead Destiny to the bedroom so I can explain some ground rules to the boys."

Mark stood there for a moment confused as Ty began to motion him towards Destiny. Mark made his way around the coffee table and interrupted the conversation by saying to Destiny with a concerned voice, "Honey? Can I talk to you for a moment?"

Destiny, confused, said, "OK," as she stood up and Mark took her by the hand and led her into the bedroom. She was actually a little relieved by the interruption as it gave her time to get control of the extreme sense of arousal she was feeling but now she was also concerned that Mark was starting to have second thoughts about all this.

Oddly enough, earlier in the evening, she had considered different things she could do if for some reason Mark wanted to back out and she still wanted to continue. She thought, *all I have to do is stall and after awhile, Mark will probably get aroused by the idea again and change his mind.*

Or, maybe I can convince him to stay in the guest bedroom if he doesn't want to watch. If that doesn't work, maybe I can get Ty to tell his friends that they have to leave and then I can convince Mark to sleep in the guest bedroom like he did last time so Ty and I can have the master bedroom to ourselves.

Then, after Mark falls asleep, Ty could call his friends back and have them sneak in the back door to our bedroom. If they stay quiet, Mark will probably never know they came back and even if he does hear them in our bedroom, as long as I don't sound like I am protesting (too much), Mark probably won't risk a confrontation with them. Instead, he will probably just let us have our fun and not do anything until after they leave. Then all I have to say is that they pressured me into doing it after he fell asleep.

Destiny felt both ashamed and turned on at the same time for considering such a deceptive plan to get Mark out of the way if she wanted to and she found she had to change her underwear more than once before eight-o-clock came around.

Now as Mark seemed to be having second thoughts, she was reminded of the naughty plan she had devised earlier in the evening. However, now she realized she lacked the courage to go through with it. Even she was beginning to have second thoughts and she felt some relief at the possibility of Mark wanting to call this off but then she also felt a sense of disappointment, too.

Destiny struggled with both the fear and excitement of what this evening had to offer but the closer she got to it the more fear seemed to be winning out. But she also knew that this was her idea. At least she had agreed to it (sort of) and now she had to live up to her commitment. As much as she wanted to, she couldn't back out now - at least not on her own accord. Her only hope now was that Mark wanted to call it off and if he didn't, she would just have to go through with it.

Mark closed the door behind her as she began concernedly, "What's wrong?"

Mark answered, "Nothing. Ty just wants to talk to the guys alone for a moment. He asked me to bring you in here."

Destiny's head lowered in disappointment as she said, "Oh. OK."

Mark asked, "Are you alright?"

Destiny tried to reply convincingly, "Yeah, I'm fine."

Mark asked, "Are you sure? You don't have to go through with this if you don't want to."

Destiny replied, "Yeah. Definitely."

Mark looked into Destiny's eyes for a moment as he sought confirmation before answering, "Good."

Destiny asked, "How about you?"

Mark answered, "Definitely."

After a moment, Mark said, "I'm going to go check on them. You alright staying here?"

Destiny answered, "Sure."

Mark said, "OK. I'll be right back," as he exited the room, closing the door behind him.

As Mark exited the bedroom he saw Ty and his friends standing in the corner of the living room in a semi-huddle as they spoke quietly. They looked over to see who it was coming out of the room and then, seeing Mark, returned to their discussion.

As Mark arrived into the semi-huddle, Ty began laying down the rules. He said to John and Sean, "OK. Number one. I understand that you guys are all worked up about tapping that ass but you need to put your dicks down for a moment and understand that Destiny is not just some call girl you found in the yellow pages... and if I see you treating her like one, I'm going to be bustin' some heads open. Understand?"

Ty paused to let that sink in before continuing, "You guys are coming on way too strong and you're going to blow it, so back off. Alright?" Ty's voice seemed a little calmer now.

Finally, feeling that he had got his boys a little more under control, Ty turned to Mark and said, as the other two listened, "OK. I want you to help facilitate this. I already know I can't keep these dogs under leash for much longer so we are going to have to skip the pleasantries and get down to it. OK?"

Mark nodded. Ty continued, "Now I want you to go back in there, bring her a bottle of wine and reassure her that everything is going to be OK... Tell her that I am going to make sure everything is all right. Make sure she drinks some wine while you talk. And once she is settled down I want you to tell her how this is going to go down."

Mark listened intently as Ty continued, "I want you two to stay in there and get things ready. Light some candles, turn on some music, and so forth and eventually you are going to invite us into the room. Tell her she isn't supposed to say anything to us, just stand there and we'll gather around her. Then tell her you are going to grab our hands, one by one, and place them on Destiny's body." They all looked at Ty questioningly as he explained, "This is a symbolic gesture to her that you approve of us touching her and it will make her feel more comfortable with moving forward."

Mark nodded as Ty gave direction. He continued, "After that, nature should take its own course." Ty smiled.

Mark nodded and said, "OK."

Ty motioned him to the bedroom.

Ty then stopped him halfway and reiterated, "Make sure she feels comfortable before you invite us in."

Mark nodded again and then grabbed the open bottle of wine on the table before proceeding to the bedroom.

Destiny had been sitting in the bedroom alone as her thoughts raced. She thought about what they were talking about, about how they were going to 'take her', she figured. It seemed pretty clear that Sean and John were interested in her and Destiny wondered how big they were. She wondered if she could handle all three of them as if she were some kind of porn queen. She thought, *I can't believe I'm going to get gang-banged by three big black guys* and her body quivered at the thought.

Destiny had imagined what it would be like to be gang-banged a few times in her life before. But now, as she sat here waiting, it all seemed so surreal. She took another sip of her wine as she wondered if she could stop them if she decided it was too much for her and she realized that she couldn't stop them, and neither could Mark. She realized that once they started, she would no longer have control over the situation and that continued to make her extremely scared and... turned on at the same time.

Mark opened the door to the bedroom and came in before closing it.

Destiny was sitting on the edge of the bed with an expectant look on her face. She asked, "Well? What's going on?"

Mark answered dismissively, "We were just talking," and he began to tell Destiny everything Ty had told him to say to her.

Destiny listened intently and was relieved to hear that Ty had given his promise that things wouldn't get out of hand. She knew Ty well enough now to trust him. Mark explained how the night was to unfold and she thought it a little strange that Mark was going to place their hands on her.

She said, "And I'm just supposed to stand there while you do this?" with a confused look on her face.

Mark explained, "Yes. It's supposed to be a symbolic gesture to you that I am OK with them touching you."

Destiny, still skeptical, replied, "OK."

Afterward, Destiny lit some candles and Mark selected some music on the clock radio beside the bed. Destiny was already on her second glass of wine when Mark looked around the room and saw everything was ready. He walked over to Destiny and said, "You ready?"

Destiny took a deep breath and said, "I think so."

Mark put his arms around her and said, "I love you."

Destiny, calmed by his voice, looked up at him and said, "I love you too," smiling.

They both sensed that this would be the last moment the two would have alone together before the 'party' started and it felt like they were saying, "See you on the other side."

The two kissed softly for a moment before Mark made his way over to the door. With his hand on the door handle, Mark stopped and looked back at Destiny, smiling. Destiny smiled back and Mark proceeded to open the door.

Mark entered the living room and found the three men sitting down talking. He stepped over to them and said to Ty, "She's ready."

Ty nodded and stood up.

They all followed him into the bedroom.

Destiny had removed her dress and was standing there wearing only her black corset, stockings and high-heel shoes.

Destiny blankly stared forward, afraid to meet their eyes as they filed in around her. Mark noticed that she had a panicked look on her face as these three towering men began to surround her.

She then fought the urge to make idle talk as the three men, grinning, gathered close around her.

Ty was standing in the middle of Sean and John and as Mark moved to grab Sean's hand and place it on Destiny, Ty moved forward and embraced Destiny as he began to kiss her.

Mark continued, putting Sean's hand on Destiny's behind and then moved around her and put John's hand on the other cheek. The two began caressing her body as Ty continued to kiss her deeply.

Destiny felt herself let go as all the hands caressed her body.

Sean and John began to remove their clothes with one hand as they explored Destiny's body with the other.

Destiny began removing Ty's clothes herself as she kissed him.

Finished, Destiny could feel Sean's cock rubbing against her side and reached out to grasp it in her hand.

She felt around with her other hand and found John's cock as she grasped it and began gently stroking both men as she felt Ty's cock pushing between her legs and Ty's tongue deep in her mouth.

Mark sat in the corner of the room and watched as these three studs pressed themselves against his wife's body, exploring her private parts with their hands and kissing her all over. He watched her stroking two of them while Ty's throbbing cock pushed between her legs. Mark noticed that Sean's cock was almost as big as Ty's and was astonished to see John's cock was even longer then Ty's.

Ty broke off his kiss and said softly to her, "You want to move up on to the bed?"

Destiny, still reaching for his kiss, eyes still closed, replied, "Sure," and she began to move back onto the bed.

Destiny moved up onto the bed as the three men continued removing their clothes. She sat on her knees in the middle of the bed smiling as she looked around expectantly at the men on all three sides of her completely undressed. Her pussy began to drip with anticipation.

Sean said to her smiling, "Have you ever been gang-banged before?"

Destiny could only respond by shaking her head as she smiled at no one in particular with growing anticipation in her face.

Sean said, "Well don't worry. We've done this before...back in our college days."

Destiny suddenly found herself envious of the subjects of their past conquests.

John said jokingly, "You could say it's our specialty," and Destiny now knew she wanted this more than anything.

The three men began to climb up on the bed from all three sides.

Destiny reached out her hands to grab their cocks and began stroking them as they began to take turns kissing her.

Still sitting in the corner, Mark began to rub his already rock hard cock through his pants.

Finally, John lay down on the bed and motioned to Destiny, who was busy stroking and kissing the other two, to get on top of him.

She mounted him in reverse cowgirl style and began to work his enormous cock inside her as he helped guide it in.

Her pussy was so wet, his cock immediately slipped deep inside her and she gasped out loud.

The three men laughed at her gasp and offered her words of encouragement.

Sean said, "There you go baby. We're going to take care of you now."

John said, "Oh yeah. She's nice and tight."

Ty replied, "Mmmm. Yes she is."

Destiny was focused now on the pain she felt deep inside her as she began to lower herself deeper onto John's cock.

Ty and Sean kneeled at her sides. Ty, feeling her breast, began to kiss her again.

Sean began sucking her other breast as one of his hands slid down her front side to massage her clit and the other hand slid down her backside. She felt Sean's finger begin to press in on her rear hole.

She gasped again as his finger entered her from behind but was quickly distracted by Ty's kiss.

Destiny gradually began to move up and down on John's cock as Sean's finger began to move in and out of her and within seconds she was experiencing her first orgasm of the night.

A few minutes later, Ty motioned John to move so he could be under her.

Destiny rose up slowly to extract John from deep inside her. Already her pussy was hurting from being stretched by John's thick cock.

As Ty moved into place, Destiny began to lower herself onto him.

Sean stopped Destiny and motioned her to turn around so that she was facing Ty.

Destiny turned around and began to take Ty inside her.

She looked Ty in the face as she continued to lower herself deeper onto him.

John was now fondling her breast and helping to support her as she lowered herself ever deeper onto Ty.

Sean crawled off the bed and made his way over to Mark. He said impatiently, "Do you have any KY? Vaseline?"

Mark thought about it for a moment and then got up to go to the bathroom behind him.

Sean returned to the bed.

Mark found the Vaseline in a drawer and brought it to Sean who was now back on the bed behind Destiny.

Destiny had lowered herself completely onto Ty's lap as she began to lean forward and kiss Ty again; Destiny loved the way Ty kissed and felt herself lost when their mouths touched.

Destiny felt hands touching her all over.

Sean applied a generous amount of Vaseline to his cock and stroked it until it was wet and covered completely. He then positioned himself directly behind Destiny and began to guide it in her ass.

Destiny looked up and leaned back when she felt Sean's cock pressing against her other hole. She said pleadingly, "I don't think I'm ready for that yet."

Sean said comfortingly, "It's OK. I'm going to be gentle," as he pushed her gently but forcibly back down to kiss Ty.

Destiny started to resist but gave in quickly as she went back to kissing Ty. Destiny had let Ty fuck her in the ass twice already and she was pretty sure she could handle Sean's cock now. But, both times Mark wasn't present for it. She hadn't even told Mark about it.

Destiny had let Mark do it to her that way before but she never really enjoyed it much when he did, so she rarely let him do it to her that way anymore. But the first night she let Ty do it to her, it felt different somehow. It hurt immensely but she really liked letting Ty do it to her for some reason.

Destiny realized she liked getting it in the ass when it was the right kind of guy and she didn't want to have to explain to Mark that for some reason he wasn't the right kind of guy.

Ty was thrusting himself slowly in and out of her with short strokes and Destiny began to feel another orgasm coming.

She felt Sean trying to enter her from behind but she resisted the urge to say anything that would distract her from her building orgasm.

As Sean's head began to enter her, she lifted her head back and made a loud moaning sound as her face seemed contracted into pain.

Destiny tried to move forward away from Sean's cock, but Sean had a hold of her by her hips and wasn't allowing her to budge.

Finally, Destiny let out a short scream as Sean suddenly entered her.

She desperately tried to pull away from Sean's firm mount as she gasped in pain. *This didn't at all feel as good as when Ty did it.* Unable to pull away she yelled, "Stop! I can't do this."

She continued to struggle as Sean said comfortingly, "It's OK. It only hurts at first. You'll get used to it."

Destiny felt immense pain as Sean began to push it in further. She begged, "Please! Stop. Let me go!" as tears began to run down her face.

Sean continued to say, "You'll get use to it. Trust us."

Crying now, Destiny looked down at Ty and begged him, "Make him stop."

Ty calmly responded, "I know it hurts but he's right. Just give it a few more moments and it will stop hurting"

Ty, seeing she wasn't convinced, said, "You can do this Destiny. Be strong. Give it a little more time and if it still hurts, I'll make him stop."

Destiny, trying to trust Ty's words, nodded as she fought back more tears.

Destiny closed her eyes and waited for the pain to subside.

Sitting in the corner, Mark watched as Sean entered Destiny. Mark heard Destiny scream and as usual, thought he should stop this but he hesitated as Sean tried to convince her that it would be OK.

Mark was on the verge of release as he watched these three large men violating his wife's body. She looked so small compared to the muscular bodies mounting her and he was reminded of the first time he saw Destiny in pain while having sex with Ty.

Mark remembered how he was about to intervene when he saw the look on her face change from pain to pleasure/pain.

Mark sat in his chair watching as he hoped the same thing would happen this time. Mark listened as Destiny cried tears of pain while Sean gradually began to move rhythmically inside of her. Mark released all over himself.

Destiny had her eyes tightly closed as Sean began to move inside of her. As he did, Destiny felt the pain subsiding a little bit. She realized that she had little control over the situation now and that the best thing she could do right now is just endure the pain as Sean had his way with her. Destiny, resigned to her fate, began to breathe methodically in short gasps and as she did, she felt the pain slowly turn to pleasure.

Mark watched as he saw Destiny begin to breathe in short controlled gasps. He remembered this sound from before and he found himself becoming erect again. Mark saw Sean respond to this as he picked up the pace and began to thrust himself deeper inside Destiny from behind. Sean was surprised that Destiny was taking his harder and deeper thrusts without protest.

Encouraged by Destiny's resolve to take it, Sean began to fuck Destiny even harder.

Destiny was lost again in the throes of an endless string of orgasms as she felt Sean violating her from behind.

She lowered herself onto Ty's chest and held him tightly in order to allow Sean deeper access to her. She could feel everything now, Ty's cock deep inside her pussy pulsing, Sean deep inside her ass as he got stiffer, even Ty's chest muscles rippling against her breast.

Destiny felt John's cock in her face and she began to stroke and suck on it as hard as she could as she began to climax.

Eventually, Destiny felt Sean go suddenly rock hard inside of her and she screamed in response.

Sean released inside of her and she could feel his cock pulsating and then, she suddenly felt Ty explode inside of her, followed shortly thereafter by John cumming in her mouth.

As the three moaned in ecstasy, Destiny was pleased to feel their juices in every orifice of her body filling her up.

Sean, feeling spent, leaned over and rested on Destiny's back with his throbbing cock still inside her.

Destiny was sandwiched between Sean and Ty's sweating bodies. Destiny could feel both of them breathing deeply as their bodies pressed against hers with their cocks shoved deep inside of her still oozing cum, John's cum in her mouth, and John's cock still throbbing in her hand as she sucked the remaining cum from the tip. Destiny felt content to spend the rest of her life in this position.

Having been licked clean, John laid down beside them on the bed as he tried to catch his breath. Destiny looked down to the corner of the room and saw Mark leaning back in his chair, eyes closed, breathing deeply as sweat ran down his face.

They all lay there in a tangle for some time as their heavy breathing subsided. Destiny could feel relief when Sean's cock started to go soft inside her. Eventually, Ty said, "So. How did you like it?"

Destiny took a moment to respond and then said wittily, "What are you guys doing tomorrow night?"

The men laughed heartily. Destiny could feel their cocks suddenly in motion inside her as they laughed and she suddenly made a quivering moan at the tickling sensation. Hearing this, the men stopped laughing before breaking out into laughter once again. Finally, she said smiling and embarrassed, "Stop. You guys keep making me cum," which caused them to laugh even harder.

Mark watched and listened from the corner of the room as they began to talk about their experience. Destiny's body was barely visible to him as she was enveloped between Sean and Ty. Mark noted that she seemed perfectly comfortable in this position as the four talked and joked about the experience.

Sean said, "See, I told you it would get better after a while."

Destiny said incredulously, "Uh Huh. It was actually quite amazing... after a while," and they all laughed again.

Sean, remembering Destiny's husband was supposed to be around somewhere, looked around to see Mark and said, "How 'bout you? You enjoy it?"

Mark, startled by being suddenly pulled into the conversation, said, "Uh Huh. It was...incredible."

The three men laughed again.

Finally, Destiny said, "Well. As much as I enjoy being in this position, I do need to get up eventually and go to the bathroom. So if you gentlemen don't mind...?"

Sean leaned back and the three began to reluctantly untangle themselves as they removed their still half erect cocks from Destiny.

Destiny, finally free from their paralyzing embrace, hurriedly made her way to the bathroom and closed the door behind her.

After she exited the room, John said, "Well, I could go for another beer."

The other two agreed and the three got up and put their pants on as Mark accompanied them back into the living room. Mark went to the kitchen and fetched four beers before returning to the living room.

John was checking his text messages as Mark passed the beers around the room. The stereo was playing music and Sean motioned to it, "What else do you got?"

Mark showed Sean the laptop he had connected to the stereo and explained that it was connected to the Internet so he could download songs if he wanted to. Sean searched for music as Mark returned to his seat.

Ty said, "By the way. Thanks for inviting us over tonight. I hope we haven't been too much of an inconvenience."

Mark replied, "No problem. I'm glad you guys came."

Sean jokingly said, "Yeah. Thanks for the beer...And letting us fuck the shit out of your wife," he laughed and the others joined in.

Mark replied unashamedly, "No problem. Thanks for giving her a good fucking. She really needed that," as he smiled.

John replied without looking, "Anytime. Anytime, my friend," as he responded to a text message.

Ty said, "Yeah. What are you guys talking about? You're flying back home tomorrow."

John responded, "Well. Anytime we're in town at least."

Sean said, "Yeah. We're going to have to come and see Ty more often now," as everybody laughed.

Destiny came out of the bedroom wearing a silk robe and carrying an empty bottle of wine. She said, "I'm out."

Mark jumped up and said, "Well have a seat and I'll open another bottle," as he dutifully headed to the basement to get another bottle.

Mark selected a bottle he thought Destiny would enjoy and returned upstairs to open it.

As he made his way to the kitchen he saw Destiny sitting on the couch with her legs crossed next to Ty. Mark opened the bottle in the kitchen and returned to the living room to fill Destiny's glass. They were talking about musical preferences as Sean played a hip-hop song Mark wasn't familiar with.

The five sat there for almost forty-five minutes talking about a variety of topics from music to the best nightclubs in town as they sipped their drinks. At one point, as John and Sean were arguing over the quality of a particular night club that Ty had taken them to the other night, Mark glanced over to Ty and Destiny who had been sitting on the couch quietly opting out of this conversation and was surprised to see them making out again. Mark tried not to stare as he returned his attention to Sean and John's dispute.

Eventually, Mark noticed them rejoining the conversation but occasionally Mark could see them out of the corner of his eye playfully kissing and touching each other as Mark absently listened to John and Sean's conversation, sometimes adding his own two cents.

A few minutes later, Mark glanced over to see Ty asking Destiny something quietly as he smiled. Mark saw Destiny smile back as she quietly answered him.

Moments later and without notice, the two stood up and Destiny began to lead Ty by the hand to the bedroom. Sean interrupted what he was saying as he noticed them leaving the room and said jokingly, "Uh oh, you guys...Ty you better save some of that for me."

Destiny smiled back at Sean and said naughtily, "Don't worry boys. There's plenty of me to go around," as the two entered the bedroom and Ty closed the door behind them.

An hour and a half had passed and Mark was in the TV room now with Sean and John as they watched MTV. Mark was watching Sean and John argue back and forth about some musician when he saw the bedroom door open.

Ty stepped out, quietly closed the door behind him, and made his way to the TV room. Sean and John stopped their conversation as they eagerly awaited Ty's report. Ty said smiling, "Who's next?"

John and Sean looked at each other and then said at the same time, "I am."

John said to Sean trying to keep his voice down, "What are you talking about? You already got to pound her booty. No. I'm next."

Sean said, "What are you talking about? She won't even be up for anything more after you stretch her cooch."

John said jokingly, "It's not my fault you two have smaller dicks then me."

Sean finally conceded to John and John finished his beer before heading into the bedroom. Mark saw the door close behind him.

About thirty minutes later, as Mark, Sean and Ty were watching a pre-recorded football game on the Sports Network, Mark began to notice a moaning sound over the noise of the TV emanating from their bedroom. Mark recognized Destiny's moans as they grew louder and more intense. They all could hear Destiny moaning off and on for another fifteen minutes and a couple of times they had made comments about it. During a commercial break her moaning suddenly got very loud as Sean declared, "Go John!" and the three laughed. Eventually, Destiny's moaning quieted.

About half an hour after the moaning stopped, the clock on the wall said 1:18AM. Mark, Ty and Sean were quietly watching MTV as they drank beers. They noticed the bedroom door opening again and watched John slink out of the bedroom, close the door quietly, and make his way to the TV room, socks and shoes in hand. He smiled and said to Sean, "You're up."

Sean responded sarcastically, "It's about time...Is she even still awake?"

John replied, "Uh, huh. She's getting tired I think but she said to send you in."

Sean left for the bedroom and closed the door behind him.

It was 2:21AM when Sean came out of the bedroom. Ty and John were done for the evening and had been ready to leave when Sean came out of the room. Sean hurriedly got dressed as Ty asked, "Is she asleep?"

Sean responded grinning, "She will be soon enough," and the others laughed in response.

The three men said their goodbyes and Mark showed them out the door. Ty stopped on his way out the door and said, "Call me when you get a chance."

Mark nodded and closed the door. He threw away the empty beer bottles before making his way to the room.

Destiny was already asleep when he arrived in the room. Mark blew out the one remaining candle and quietly slipped into bed. He noticed the bed sheets were full of wet spots especially in the middle of the bed and thought they definitely would need to wash the sheets tomorrow. He snuggled up behind Destiny and noticed she had already removed her corset but still had her stockings on. She stirred and Mark said, "Did you have fun tonight?"

Destiny replied sleepily, "Uh huh," and then added humorously, "but my pussy and ass hurt."

Mark chuckled and said, "I bet." Finally he said softly, "I love you."

She replied back, "I love you too," and the two slipped into unconsciousness.

Chapter 11: Excursions Into The Unknown

Mark and Destiny continued to have Ty come over from time to time and eventually they fell into a routine. At first, Ty would usually come over on Friday nights but sometimes that would conflict with other plans that either he had or they had and they would have to go weeks without seeing him. Then Ty started coming over on weeknights instead. Eventually, Thursdays became the night of preference and Ty would come over for a couple hours so Ty and Destiny could enjoy some playtime together. Sometimes Mark would watch them play and sometimes he would just let them enjoy some private time together as he spent the evening watching TV in the other room. Sometimes just after Ty left, Mark would suddenly be overcome with the desire to eat Destiny's pussy and he would lap up all her juices before thrusting himself inside her and filling her with his cum.

Gradually Ty became an extension of their relationship. Both Mark and Destiny felt Ty's visits provided something that had always been missing in their relationship. For Destiny, she was able to satisfy a unique sexual need that Mark was unable to provide her with, while still maintaining the loving relationship she had with Mark. For Mark, he was able to experience a level of sexual gratification while watching Ty and Destiny's couplings that he never thought was possible and it made the love and affection he felt for Destiny stronger than ever before. Destiny enjoyed the new, affectionate Mark and their bond seemed to grow stronger after each visit from Ty. They both wondered how they had managed before meeting Ty.

One day, several months into their relationship with Ty, Mark was preparing for a business trip the next week. He would be out of town for a whole week and Wednesday was Destiny's birthday. Mark felt bad that he wouldn't be there for her birthday and so he decided to contact Ty to see if he would be available to take Destiny out to dinner for her birthday and then afterwards come over to the house for some fun together. Ty agreed.

That evening while Mark was packing for his trip the next morning, he said to Destiny in a matter-of-fact tone of voice, "Oh, by the way, I hope you haven't made any plans for your birthday next Wednesday."

Destiny said, "No. Why?"

Mark responded, "Because I asked Ty to come over at six and take you out to dinner."

Destiny said incredulously, "What?"

Mark just continued as he said, "Make sure you show him a good time."

Destiny was silently stunned. She wasn't sure if Mark was kidding or serious at first. Finally she decided to play along and see as she said obediently, "OK."

Mark didn't show any reaction to her response. Instead Mark said, "Have you seen my new dress shoes?"

Destiny hesitated for a moment before saying, "They're on the top shelf in the hall closet."

Mark went to get the shoes.

Destiny realized at that point, Mark was indeed serious about Ty coming over to take her out to dinner and she felt herself becoming wet at the prospects.

Destiny left work a little early that Wednesday evening. All week she was both excited and apprehensive about her coming 'Date' with Ty. She had never been seen in public with her black lover before and the fact that Mark was away on a business trip made it seem very naughty.

Destiny was a little nervous. It even felt a little like cheating but then she remembered that Mark had actually told her to go out with

Ty, not asked her but told her. He had even told her to make sure Ty had a good time and Mark could only mean one thing by that. Destiny convinced herself that she was just obeying her husband's wishes.

Destiny also felt strangely aroused by the idea of strangers seeing her with her tall, dark and handsome lover. Going out with Ty was a little risqué, too, because someone she knew could happen to see her and think she was having a secret affair behind Mark's back and taking that risk somehow made it even more arousing.

Destiny had wondered over the week where Ty had planned to take her for dinner. She thought if it happened to be one of the places that her and Mark frequented, it could be a little awkward with the wait staff.

Destiny took a shower, got dressed and put on make-up in preparation for the evening. She decided to wear the elegant yet sexy tight red dinner dress she rarely got to wear.

As she was finishing with her make-up in the bathroom, she heard the doorbell ring. She went to the door and opened it to see Ty standing there dressed for the occasion. Ty looked very handsome in his slacks and tight shirt. Destiny invited him in as she said smiling, "Hello."

Ty responded smiling, "Hello beautiful."

The two embraced and kissed each other. Destiny was keenly aware that Mark was thousands of miles away and that this was the first time she greeted Ty at the door without Mark somewhere close by.

Destiny broke off and said apologetically, "I'm sorry. I'm still not ready."

Ty responded, "Don't worry. Take your time. I'm a little early anyway."

Destiny smiled and then said, "I just need a couple more minutes. Make yourself comfortable."

As she headed back towards the bathroom she asked, "Where are we going anyway?"

Ty responded, "I made reservations for us at Jack's."

Jack's was a high-end steak house across town and Destiny was relieved that it wasn't one of her and Mark's regular places. She was also glad she decided to really dress up because Jack's was a very classy place.

Destiny finished her make-up, grabbed a coat from the closet and the two headed out the door to Ty's BMW.

Although Ty had made reservations, they still had to wait a couple minutes to be seated. Destiny had held Ty's arm as they went in and now, as they stood there waiting to be seated with several other couples, Destiny held on to Ty closely again. She couldn't understand why, but part of her really wanted others to see them together and know that she was probably going to be fucked by her black stud later in the evening. Moments later, the hostess called their name.

She sat them in a booth and Destiny noticed the hostess, who couldn't be more than seventeen years old, subtly blushing as she said to Ty, "Your waitress should be with you in just a moment. In the meantime, is there anything else I could get you?" with a flirtatious smile on her face. Ty smiled back and said, "No, thank you. We'll be fine."

Destiny enjoyed their dinner together but she found it hard to think about anything else but sex. Destiny consumed three cocktails in a very short amount of time as they discussed a variety of mundane topics.

Destiny was reminded of when she was single and the mix of anxiety and excitement she would feel when going out with someone on a first date. Except this time it was a little different.

This time she knew she would be having sex with this man afterward and she also knew that it would be great sex.

They finished dinner and Ty paid the bill. Destiny held on to Ty's arm again as they made their way through the dining room and she noticed a number of married white men, whom she had noticed occasionally glancing over to look at them while that sat in the booth, were now watching them as they left. Destiny started to feel incredibly naughty as she found herself adding a little extra swing to her hips as they walked out of the restaurant and out to Ty's car.

Destiny was feeling incredibly horny now. Ty opened the passenger door for her and as he got in on the other side, Destiny found herself reaching over and grabbing his crotch as she began to kiss him passionately.

Destiny was aware they were still in the parking lot at Jack's but it was getting dark and there wasn't anybody else around and she found she didn't really care anyway. She just knew that she had to feel his monster cock inside her mouth right now.

Destiny began unzipping Ty's trousers. She pulled his already erect cock out and thrust it in her mouth as she stroked it with a free hand.

Destiny vigorously worked Ty's cock in and out of her mouth while gripping it tightly.

She tried to bring Ty all the way inside her mouth and down her throat but was discouraged by the fact that she couldn't find the right angle to force his cock down her throat. She coughed as she tried and then finally gave up as she went back to vigorously stroking him. She thought to herself, *I'll try again later on the couch back at the house.*

As Ty approached climax, he grabbed a handful of Destiny's hair and began thrusting her head down on his cock.

Destiny moaned approvingly.

Then Destiny heard a noise that sounded like someone getting into the car parked next to them. At this point she didn't care if someone had seen them and if to prove it, she began moaning much louder.

Ty said, "Shhhh... There are people getting into the car next to us."

Destiny suddenly realized she actually wanted someone to see her sucking on Ty's big black cock like a dirty slut. She continued to moan loudly.

After a few more minutes, Ty shot his load deep down Destiny's throat and Destiny finished diligently licking his cock clean.

Eventually, Destiny leaned back over into her seat and smiling said, "Satisfied?"

Ty, still trying to catch his breath, managed to say, "Yeah... For now," and then added smiling, "I think they liked it, too," as he motioned to the truck parked next to them on his side.

Destiny looked over and saw a big truck parked next to them. From the passenger seat where she was sitting, she could not see into the truck's windows. Destiny leaned over into Ty's lap and looked out his window to see a group of men in the king cab truck looking intently out the windows into Ty's window. Some guys on the other side of the truck were even leaning over to catch a view.

Destiny recognized the men from the restaurant. They had been sitting at a table by the bar and she had noticed them glancing over at her and Ty as they walked by on the way out of the dining room area.

Destiny grinned naughtily at the men staring at her and saw them begin to laugh as she leaned back over into the passenger seat smiling to herself.

Ty started the car and they drove away.

Destiny wondered to herself how much they must have seen while she was giving Ty a blowjob.

Destiny was amazed at herself. At how much she had changed. Just a few months ago, she wouldn't even consider giving her husband a blowjob in such a public place. Now here she was, a married white woman giving a blow job to a big black guy in his car while other men watched her do it. Destiny realized that she was really starting to like it when she was watched by other white men while she fucked her black stud. It made Destiny feel real slutty and that really got her off.

As they pulled out of the parking lot, Ty said grinning, "Well. That was pretty interesting."

Destiny said apologetically, "I know. I'm sorry." Feeling a little embarrassed and ashamed now, she continued, "I don't know what got into me. I'm not normally like that... I swear!" Ty interrupted saying, "You don't have to apologize. I enjoyed it."

Destiny replied, "Really? Good. I just don't want you to get the wrong idea about me or anything. I've never done anything like that before. Not even with Mark."

Ty said sincerely, "I believe you."

Destiny smiled quietly and looked forward as Ty drove them back to her house.

When they arrived, Ty jumped out of the car and opened the door for her. As Destiny began to walk toward the house, Ty reached into the back seat and grabbed a bottle of wine and a gift-wrapped box. Destiny unlocked the front door as Ty arrived by her side. She saw the gift in his hand and smiled broadly as she asked excitedly, "Is that for me?"

Ty answered, "Of course. It's your birthday isn't it?" as they walked into the living room.

Destiny said, "You didn't have to do that."

Ty raised the bottle of wine in the other hand and asked, "Do you have a bottle opener?"

Destiny answered, "Uh Huh," as she made her way to the kitchen to fetch it.

Ty followed her.

Destiny grabbed two wine glasses from the cabinet as Ty opened the bottle. Ty poured two glasses and handed one to her as he said, "To your birthday!"

Destiny smiled as they clinked glasses and drank.

Ty said, "Now for your present," and handed her the gift.

Destiny smiled as she put her glass down and began opening it. She stopped half way, turned to Ty and kissed him. Then she said, "Thanks," smiling into his eyes as she proceeded to unwrap her present.

Inside she was stunned to find what appeared to be an S&M outfit. It looked like a teddy as she held it up but it was made entirely of thin leather straps that crisscrossed each other and attached to metal rings at various points. She said, "Wow. That's interesting." She also found what appeared to be a set of leather restraints and handcuffs, and a leather whip, and a leather clad paddle. Destiny said "Hmmm," as she began to realize that the entire box was filled with Bondage and S&M gear. She also noticed that all the items were of high quality materials for serious S&M players. Not the cheap kind of 'Bondage Kit' that couples buy on a whim and is made of cheap simulated leather stuff that falls apart the first time you use it. No, this was the real stuff.

Destiny was still smiling as she inventoried the items but she was speechless now as she wasn't sure how she should react to such a gift.

Finally, Ty said, "Just so you know. I asked Mark if it was OK to buy you this kind of gift beforehand."

Destiny was stunned to hear this but she continued to smile as she said, "You did? And he was OK with it?"

Ty replied, "Actually, he thought it was a great idea." Ty continued, "As a matter of fact, I let him know that I have had some experience with dominating women in the past and that, for some time now, I have been interested in trying a few things with you. I asked him if he would be OK with that."

Destiny's heart raced as she suddenly realized that Ty had bought this gift for her and Ty to use, not for Mark and her. Destiny's face began to turn red with excitement and she was unable to look Ty in the face as she asked, "And what did Mark say?"

Ty replied deviously, "He thought you might enjoy a few lessons in discipline and that tonight would be a good night for me to start your training."

Destiny was taken aback. She was shocked at how the evening's planned activities had taken an unimaginable new direction and Destiny was stunned to learn that Mark had approved of all this. Destiny began to feel a little faint as she considered the possibilities.

Destiny imagined for a moment Ty tying her up in their bed, of Ty spanking her and forcing her to suck on his cock with her hands cuffed behind her back. Destiny imagined Ty dominating her like she had never been dominated before. Destiny felt ashamed at the fact that these images really turned her on.

Finally, Destiny put away her shame as she surrendered to her desires. Destiny knew she wanted to be Ty's slave for the night more than anything else right now and she felt her knees weakening at the prospect.

Finally, Ty asked, smile fading, "Well. Do you like your present?"

Destiny answered enthusiastically, "Yes... I do...I love it!" and continued, "It's just...Wow! I'm surprised. I wasn't expecting this... At all!"

Ty asked, "Do you think you're ready for this?"

Destiny thought for a moment and then replied, "Yes! Definitely!"

Destiny, not knowing what else to say, threw herself at Ty and began kissing him.

She finally pulled away and reached for her glass as she said, "I'm going to need a few more of these, though."

They laughed for a moment before Ty said, "Yeah. I wasn't sure how you would feel about this," and then more seriously added, "I've actually thought a lot about tying you up... And other things."

Destiny felt a shiver run down her spine at Ty's words. Finally she said plainly, "Really?" and she took another gulp from her glass.

Ty said, "Yes I have," and continued, "I've always kind of been into sexual dominance play."

He added further, "You could say it's a hobby of mine," as he grinned into Destiny's face.

Destiny was unable to grin back at Ty as she was fighting to keep control of herself, to keep from fainting. Every time she thought about the implications of what Ty was saying, she became so suddenly aroused that her knees felt weak and she had to try and get the images out of her head before she collapsed to the floor.

As Destiny tried to keep her cool, she became suddenly aware that she was continuing to sip from her glass that had long since been emptied. She reached for the bottle and with shaky hands, filled her glass to the top and it began to overflow. Completely flustered now, she said, "Whoa! ...I'm getting a little carried away here," as she laughed.

Destiny reached for a kitchen towel to wipe up the spillage.

Ty began to say, "Of course. If it's too much for you right now..."

Destiny interrupted, "No! It's fine...I mean...I need to sit down is all."

Destiny abruptly made her way to the living room couch and half way there, changed directions to the bedroom and said, "Actually, I need to go to the bathroom, if you don't mind."

All the while Ty smiled as he recognized that Destiny was quite rattled and clearly turned on by what Ty had proposed.

He called out, "Of course," and Destiny added, "I'll be just a minute. Don't go anywhere. OK?"

Destiny closed the door to the bathroom behind her and supported herself by her arms as she leaned heavily against the counter top trying to keep her balance. She took a deep breath and let it out as she looked at herself in the mirror. She realized she needed to sit down for a moment and turned to the walk-in closet where there was a padded square seat she could sit on. She sat down and decided it wasn't enough, that she needed to lean back and then felt herself sliding off the seat to sit on the floor as she leaned back on the unstable seat. Her face felt flush with waves of coolness spreading over it as she fought to get control over herself.

Eventually, Destiny began to feel better as she got used to the images swimming around in her head. Images of her helplessly tied up as Ty had his every way with her. As she slowly came back to her senses, she momentarily laughed out loud as she realized she had never been affected this deeply before. Not even close. She marveled at how turned on she had been and how she actually was on the verge of fainting.

Destiny had thought about S&M before in her life and found it mildly arousing to her. But now, as the S&M experience was imminent, and with Ty being the one to dominate her, she was overwhelmingly turned on. She realized that between this and the experience in the car just a few hours ago, that she had somehow changed over the past few months. Destiny's sex drive was now in overdrive in a way she never imagined possible.

Suddenly it occurred to Destiny that she had been sitting there in the closet for a long time and Ty was no doubt wondering what had happened to her. Destiny got to her feet and made her way to the bathroom mirror. She looked herself over, decided to put some lipstick on real quick and took a deep breath before opening the door to return to the living room.

Ty was sitting on the couch refilling his glass of wine when Destiny walked in. Destiny said, "Sorry about that. I had to freshen up a little bit."

Ty replied, "No problem," as he held out her glass of wine.

Destiny sat down beside him and took a deep gulp. She realized that the wine was beginning to have the desired effect on her as she finally started to relax and be able to talk about the experience that Ty was proposing. Destiny said, "Let me look at that stuff again," as she rose up and went over to the kitchen counter to fetch the box of gifts she received.

She returned to the couch and began to go over the items a little more thoroughly.

She held up the teddy made of leather straps and said smiling, "I really like this," and added jokingly, "I'm not sure how it goes on though."

Ty replied grinningly, "Well, I can help you with that."

Destiny met his eyes and smiled as she said, "Thanks. But I'm sure I'll figure it out."

She then reached for the leather restraints and said approvingly, "Interesting."

Ty responded, "I'm glad you like it."

Not able to contain herself any longer, Destiny reached back for the teddy and said, "Maybe I should go and put this on now," as she looked at Ty for his approval.

Ty nodded and said, "If you ready."

Destiny took another deep chug from her glass and said, "I'll be back in a moment then," as she got up and made her way to the bedroom.

Before she made it there, Ty said, "Just a minute."

Destiny stopped and turned.

Ty motioned her back to him. Standing in front of her he asked softly, "Do you know what a safe word is?"

Destiny responded smiling, "Yes. I think so."

Ty replied, "Good. You safe word is 'Mercy'. Understand?"

Destiny replied, "Yes."

Ty said, "OK. You can go get dressed now."

Still smiling, Destiny turned and walked towards the bedroom door. She closed the door behind her.

Destiny found herself pausing occasionally to take a deep breath as she undressed herself. She also found her underwear was soaking wet as she took them off. Once she put the outfit on, she began to see how sexy it was as she looked at herself in the mirror.

Destiny was feeling overwhelmed again and realized she was not going to make it through the rest of the evening this way. She realized that part of the reason she had been so aroused was because she had not had sex for almost a week now.

Destiny decided the arousal was too much and for the first time ever, she decided to pleasure herself before having sex. Destiny, wearing this new outfit, made sure the bathroom door was locked and then went into the walk-in closet. She positioned herself on the floor leaning back against the chair with her legs spread in a way where she could see herself in the full-length mirror. As she looked at herself in the mirror wearing this incredibly sexy bondage outfit, Destiny massaged her clit.

Destiny had only been playing with herself for a couple of minutes before she began to orgasm. When she was finished, she felt a little more calm and able to function as she cleaned herself up. Finally, she returned to the living room.

Ty was inspecting the whip in his hand when Destiny returned to the living room. She said, "What do you think?"

Ty stood up and smiled approvingly at Destiny as she slowly walked towards him.

Destiny kissed Ty softly and then found herself saying, "I'm ready master," as she smiled up into his face.

Ty smiled back and without a word, grabbed her arm firmly and began to lead her forcefully back to the bedroom with the box of items in his other hand.

Destiny was stunned momentarily as Ty effortlessly dragged her back to the bedroom with his unshakable grip on her arm and closed the door behind them.

Inside the bedroom, Destiny noticed that Ty had transformed into a different person. A side of Ty she had never seen. As Ty began to roughly bind her hands and feet, Destiny was beginning to feel very scared.

Finally, Destiny found the courage to let go and let Ty decide her fate as she submitted to his every command and punishment.

That night Destiny felt a mixture of pain and pleasure that she never thought could go together.

At times she screamed loudly as she begged Ty to stop. At times, it hurt so good she wanted it to stop. She had even prepared to use her safe word telling herself, *I think I can take this but if he goes any further, I'm going to say it.*

Yet, each time Ty would go further, she found she could take just a little bit more and always, she found pleasure with the pain. When it was all over, she never once uttered the word 'Mercy'.

Mark had finished work for the day and was now back in his hotel room watching the local news station. He noticed the time on the alarm clock next to his bed. Mark was in a different time zone and had to do a mental calculation to figure out the time back home. He realized that Ty had probably already picked Destiny up for dinner. Mark shut the TV off at that point as he began to imagine the possible activities that Ty and Destiny were engaged in as he began to stroke his cock.

Mark had planned to spend this evening masturbating in his room as he imagined all the things that Ty and Destiny were doing at that very moment in time. Mark ran a number of scenarios through his head as he played the evening out in real time and came on himself twice before falling asleep.

When Mark had called Ty last week to see if he could take Destiny out while Mark was out of town and Ty had agreed, Ty had asked Mark if Destiny had ever tried any S&M. Mark had told Ty that she hadn't (at least not to Mark's knowledge). Ty then asked if he could introduce Destiny to the experience. Mark considered what Ty was suggesting for a moment as Ty went on to explain that he had some prior experience in dominating woman. Ty said from his experience, he was pretty good at sensing things in women and that he had sensed some submissive tendencies in Destiny that Ty thought should be explored.

When Mark imagined Destiny in bondage as Ty dominated her he became suddenly very aroused. Mark had only fleetingly considered playing some S&M games with Destiny before, but it seemed a little silly. Mark sometimes would spank Destiny on the ass as he fucked her from behind and although she would moan approvingly, Mark still felt it seemed a little silly and couldn't bring himself to continue spanking her without breaking into laughter at the whole thing. Mark just wasn't that kind of person. *But maybe Destiny was that kind of person and he just never knew it.*

As Ty talked, Mark thought he made a lot of sense. Mark realized he was probably not the right person to explore S&M with

Destiny but maybe Ty was and the thought of Destiny becoming Ty's sex slave was very erotic to Mark. Finally, Mark agreed to let Ty introduce Destiny to S&M. Ty had also suggested that it might be hard for Destiny to slip into the role of a submissive if Mark was actually nearby on the first few encounters.

Ty went on to say that while Mark was out of town it might be the best time for Ty to successfully introduce Destiny to this new experience. Furthermore, if Ty was successful with Destiny and she enjoyed being dominated, Ty said he would show Mark how to dominate Destiny as well. Mark agreed to let Ty try his hand at dominating his wife while he was away on this trip.

Mark awoke later in his hotel room. He looked at the clock beside the bed and realized he had been asleep for hours. Again, he imagined how Destiny and Ty's evening had progressed thus far.

Mark wondered how Destiny reacted when she opened the present that Ty said he was going to get for her.

Mark realized that she must have opened the present hours ago now and Mark expected if Ty's advances for S&M play hadn't gone over well with her then Destiny would eventually call Mark to tell him all about Ty's S&M present.

Destiny hadn't called yet and it was late which to Mark meant Ty had succeeded in getting her to explore S&M with him.

Mark realized that Destiny was probably well into the evening's main event.

As Mark thought about the condition Destiny was probably in right now, this very second, as Ty dominated her, he stroked himself until he came again before falling back to sleep.

Destiny awoke in the middle of the night to find Ty asleep on his back beside her in Mark and hers bed. Her behind was throbbing with red hot pain and she became dimly aware of other parts of her anatomy that seemed to be on fire, too.

Destiny began to replay some of the evening's events in her head and as she did, she began to smile to herself. Feeling completely gratified, she slowly rolled over onto Ty's side.

Destiny pulled herself close and put her arm and leg over him as she rested her head on his masculine chest. Destiny fell back to sleep with a broad smile on her face.

The next morning, Destiny stirred as she heard someone coming out of the bathroom and getting back into bed. It was Ty, she saw. Destiny smiled as she snuggled up against Ty. Ty turned to her smiling and asked in his usual deep voice, "You enjoy last night?"

Destiny smiled deeper as she took a breath and answered, "Uh Huh."

Ty said, "Good."

They smiled into each other's face for a moment before Ty said, "I've got to go to work soon."

Destiny looked at the clock across from him and saw it was 6:30AM.

Destiny said sleepily, "No. Not yet."

Destiny was already starting to feel aroused again just at the sight of Ty there in her bedroom.

Ty said, "I'm already running late," as he moved in to kiss her.

They began to kiss more passionately and Destiny's hand probed down under the sheets to find Ty's cock already rock hard.

Slowly, Destiny crawled on top of Ty and leaned back as she straddled him.

Destiny struggled to get Ty's hard cock underneath her and into her waiting pussy. She found that she had to slide one knee forward and stand on her foot until she could get the head of Ty's cock under her pussy and then slide her knee back as she slowly worked him into her.

Destiny realized she had never had to do this when she straddled Mark but then Mark's penis was much smaller than Ty's. Destiny tried to remember how she was able to reach climax with Mark's small penis in her now that she had grown accustomed to Ty's enormous cock filling her up inside. Destiny realized that although she still enjoyed making love to Mark, she needed a cock like Ty's in order to reach full orgasm and Destiny was glad that she had a sharing husband like Mark that was willing to make that accommodation for her.

Destiny moved slowly at first but gradually her rhythm picked up speed and intensity.

She fucked Ty for fifteen minutes before Ty exploded in her.

She lay back down in bed as Ty got up to put his clothes on. Destiny watched.

They kissed one more time before Ty, making his way to the door said smiling, "Call me."

Destiny smiled back and said, "I will."

Ty left.

Destiny finally got up realizing she was also late for work.

In the bathroom, she looked in the mirror and for the first time saw and felt all the bruises on her body. Destiny had bruises around her wrists and ankles. She turned to see her ass covered in red welts and as she touched them, they began to sting. Destiny was shocked as she looked even closer in the mirror to see she had lash marks across her back, torso, breasts and even pelvis.

Destiny couldn't remember why she had wanted to be abused in this way by Ty but she remembered that she was really turned on by it at the time.

Destiny replayed the evening in her head as she showered and got ready for work being careful to conceal all the welts and bruises that had formed on her. Destiny remembered the immense pain she had experienced and she remembered the immense pleasure that came with it. As she remembered the pleasure, Destiny began to want more.

Later that evening, Mark called and asked Destiny how the evening went. Destiny said she was still feeling exhausted from the experience and was too tired to talk about it right now. She didn't offer any details other than they had a great evening. Mark sensed that she wasn't ready to talk about it yet and so he changed the subject. Mark returned home the next day.

As the days passed, Mark wanted to ask Destiny about that evening but each time he did, Destiny seemed uncomfortable talking about it and tried to change the subject. However, Mark did notice that Destiny had incurred a number of bruises and welts while he was out of town which confirmed to him that she and Ty did do something that night but Mark pretended not to notice the marks.

Destiny was uncomfortable talking to Mark about what had happened that night with Ty. Destiny knew that Ty had already told Mark what his intentions were and that Mark was supportive of it but when it came to actually sharing the details of the night with Mark, Destiny felt too embarrassed and even ashamed to discuss it. Destiny didn't want to have to tell Mark how Ty had bound her, how he had tortured her into submission and most importantly, how she had so thoroughly enjoyed all of it and even begged for more in the end. Destiny decided that what she and Ty had experienced that night should be kept between them and not shared with Mark and Destiny hoped Mark would be OK with that. Furthermore, Destiny decided, if Ty wanted to explore this kind of sexuality further with her and Mark was OK with not having to know all the details, she would give it serious consideration.

Mark was concerned that something bad had happened that night and that was the reason why Destiny seemed unwilling to talk about it. Mark decided to call Ty to find out what actually happened. Ty explained that everything went as planned and that Destiny definitely fell right into the role of a submissive. He did not offer any more details than that. However, Ty explained that some women have a hard time talking about it for the first few times because most women feel ashamed at allowing themselves to be humiliated like that, especially when it means acknowledging to others and to themselves that they can actually get-off on being forced into submission. Ty said it may take a few more sessions before Destiny is ready to share this side of herself with Mark. Ty also said that when she is ready to share this side with Mark then Ty can begin teaching Mark how to dominate her, too, but until that time comes, Mark shouldn't press her too much for details. Mark accepted Ty's guidance on this matter and stopped pressing Destiny for details about that night.

Over the next two months, Mark and Destiny meet with Ty six times for the usual encounter. Then Destiny learned that Mark had to go on another business trip.

A couple of days later Mark said to her, "I was thinking of having Ty come over again while I'm gone. Maybe you guys could have a little fun like last time. What do you think?"

Destiny had been wondering if Mark was going to say something about this. Ever since she learned that Mark had to go on another business trip she had been thinking about that night when Ty introduced her to S&M. Part of her was afraid to try it again because she had spent two weeks afterwards convincing herself that she was not that kind of person. But the other part of her secretly hoped it would happen again. Finally, Destiny said passively, "OK."

Mark made the necessary arrangements with Ty.

Again, Ty came over while Mark was out of town and Destiny submitted to him completely. From then on, when ever Mark would go out of town on business, Mark and Ty would make the same arrangements and each time, Destiny would get another 'lesson' in submission. Afterwards, Mark wouldn't press Destiny for any details about their private encounters and Destiny didn't offer any. Mark would simply ask, "How was your night with Ty?" to which Destiny would usually answer dismissively, "We had fun," which usually ended the topic.

However, Mark often found bruises and rashes on Destiny's body when he returned home. Destiny didn't offer any explanation for these things and Mark pretended not to notice. Sometimes though, Mark would talk to Ty and he would provide a few details of their progress. The three of them still continued to have their usual 'meetings' together where Mark was allowed to pleasure himself as he watched the two of them perform but over time, Mark had come to accept the fact that when he was away, Destiny and Ty enjoyed some 'special' nights together and that Mark didn't necessarily need to know all the intimate details from them. Mark even found pleasure in the idea that Ty and Destiny had a few secrets of their own.

Over time, Mark even began to enjoy the idea of Destiny and Ty engaging in occasional private interludes whenever she felt she needed some private play time with Ty or if circumstances prevented Mark from joining in. Mark realized that he trusted Destiny with Ty and that he wanted her to enjoy herself even if sometimes Mark was unable to be a part of it.

One Monday morning while both Mark and Destiny were at work, Destiny called Mark to talk about the difficult day she was already having. Destiny seemed stressed out to Mark and at one point Destiny sighed and said, "Too bad it isn't Thursday."

Mark understood what she meant by that. Thursdays were usually Destiny and Ty's play night and most times Mark would get to watch them as they coupled. Unfortunately, Ty was unable to make it last week and it had been almost two weeks since they had been able to get together.

Mark understood that with the day she was having, Destiny could really use a good fuck right now. Mark considered trying to meet Destiny back home for lunch so he could give her one but he was booked solid with meetings today and there was no way he could meet up with her.

The thought crossed Mark's mind that they could call Ty and see if he would be interested in coming over tonight but Mark remembered that they had agreed to go over to a friend's house after work for dinner and that it would be difficult to get home at a reasonable time. Destiny also remembered this commitment, which is why she hadn't suggested the idea of inviting Ty over tonight herself.

Mark considered possible solutions and finally said, "I wonder what Ty is doing for lunch today?"

Mark waited for a moment and then continued, "You should give him a call and see if he would be interested in swinging by the house for lunch today."

Destiny responded holding the phone close to her mouth so that eavesdroppers could not hear, "Really? I hadn't thought of that. But what about you? Can you come home for lunch?"

Mark really wished that he could come home for lunch and watch as her and Ty went at it as he could use a little sexual release himself right now. However, he realized that even if he could it would probably only make things more complicated and after all, this was something that Destiny needed right now. It was about her not him. Finally he said, "Unfortunately, I have a meeting to go to."

Destiny was silent before Mark continued under his breath and holding his own phone close to his mouth said, "You know, I don't always have to be there if you guys just want to hook-up for a quickie or something... or even if you guys just want some private time. I'm actually OK with that."

Destiny was silent for a moment before she said, "Really? You would be OK with that?"

Mark replied, "Sure. Just as long as you guys don't completely forget about me," he teased.

Destiny responded affectionately, "I would never forget about you."

They were silent for a moment before Mark said in a normal voice again, "So, why don't you give him a call and see if you could meet for lunch."

Destiny responded appreciatively, "Maybe I will."

After a moment of silence Destiny said, "I love you."

Mark replied, "I love you too," and the two hung up.

That evening Mark went straight from work to their friend's house for dinner. He hadn't had a chance to call Destiny since they last talked in the morning and he had completely forgotten about his suggestion to her for a lunchtime 'fix'. Mark expected to find Destiny there but she hadn't arrived yet. She was a little late, they all noticed, but when she walked in the door, Mark could almost see a radiance coming off her and only Mark knew why. Although Mark hadn't had a chance to ask her if she actually met with Ty at lunch, he could tell by the cheerful presence she brought to the party that she had recently received a good fucking.

Mark felt extremely fortunate to be married to such a beautiful woman as he imagined for a moment just how beautiful and sexy she was when Ty mounted her and when she began to moan with that pain/pleasure sound that only Ty's enormous black cock and dominant nature could bring out in her. And Mark relished the fact that he was the only one in the room who knew this side of Destiny.

Chapter 12: Epilogue

Mark and Destiny had been seeing Ty for a little over a year, when Destiny happened to win a free trip to Las Vegas on a radio show. Unfortunately, Mark wasn't able to go on the available dates so he suggested to her to invite Ty to go instead. Destiny invited Ty and he accepted.

Afterward, Destiny had reported that they had a wonderful time dancing but mostly they spent a lot of time having sex in the hotel room. Destiny said that they even had sex in one of the hotel's hot tubs one night and that another couple happened to walk in on them as Destiny was sitting on Ty's lap.

Destiny recounted the story to Mark later. It was later in the evening and the hotel's pool and hot tubs were technically closed. But Ty and Destiny had snuck down to the hot tub anyway. No one else was there and they found a secluded hot tub that they had all to themselves. It was dark and they tried to remain quiet.

Destiny had been fondling Ty and she eventually removed the bottom piece to her bikini. Destiny was sitting on Ty's cock and it was shoved deep inside her. She was moaning softly and her eyes were closed when she heard voices very near to them.

Destiny quickly regained her composure as a couple abruptly appeared before them with towels in hand. Destiny said, "Hello," as she tried to pretend she was just sitting on her husband/boyfriend's lap.

Unaware of what she and Ty were up to, the couple replied, "Good evening. Mind if we join you?" as they entered the hot tub.

Destiny had no choice but to say, "Sure. No Problem."

Destiny tried to maintain her composure as she asked them where they were from and the four engaged in a friendly conversation.

Destiny was glad that the underwater light wasn't on but she was starting to get concerned about the time left on the jets. If the bubbles shut off, they might be able to see that she wasn't wearing anything below the waist and neither was Ty. Eventually, she asked the man who was sitting on the edge of the hot tub if he could go and reset the timer before the jets shut off and was relieved when he did without asking her why.

Occasionally, Ty would jostle her a little bit as he reached for his drink and Destiny would gasp unexpectedly.

She tried to explain to the couple that she had been experiencing muscles spasms lately which is why they decided to take a dip in the hot tub.

Eventually, the couple moved to the corner to sit and talk amongst themselves about tomorrow night's plans.

Relieved of her social responsibilities, Destiny closed her eyes and began to focus on Ty's cock again as it pushed deep inside her.

After awhile, she became oblivious to her surroundings and she began to quietly orgasm again.

At some time later, Ty caught her as she began to faint.

When she came to, she noticed the other couple had left at some point and that it was just Ty and herself in the hot tub now. She hadn't known how long she had been in that condition or what sounds she may have made before the other couple left.

Ty had told her that she was fine...for awhile and then she began to make soft noises that he suspected the other couple could hear. The couple casually left the hot tub, dried off quickly and politely said goodbye. Ty said Destiny didn't even respond to their farewell and that he had to respond for her. Ty said that they must have realized at that point that the two were having sex as they hurried away.

Ty and Destiny returned to their room and after a short nap, she found the energy to go to a nightclub. They danced late into the night and made quite a stir on the dance floor as all the white guys in the club stared at her envious of Ty. Eventually, they returned to their room and had sex again before falling asleep in each other's arms.

Destiny had many fond memories of that trip. However, she remembered missing Mark more than anything and found herself calling him every chance she could. She couldn't seem to wait to get home. That's when Destiny realized that her relationship with Ty could never replace what she had with Mark.

She knew that Mark's love for her was unconditional and that he truly enjoyed seeing her explore her sexuality with other men. For Mark, seeing her pleasured by another man brought Mark to new heights of pleasure himself. They continued to meet with Ty on a regular basis but even though Destiny found her sexual needs fulfilled with Ty in ways she never imagined, she knew that Ty didn't love her unconditionally like Mark did and that Ty had no interest in being tied to just one person anyway. Nor did she love Ty in the way she loved Mark.

Destiny did continue to share a special bond with Ty separate from Mark and they even continued to privately engage in more S&M play on occasion without Mark's knowledge. But that was different, she thought. Ty and hers relationship was purely sexual in nature which somehow made it possible for her to fall into a role of complete submission with Ty. She could never do that with Mark, she realized, and she never wanted to either. There were some things that she would let Ty do to her that she would never let Mark do.

Mostly though, Destiny thought of her relationship with Ty as a special friend who enabled her to reach a higher level of climax than she could achieve with Mark and this in turn enabled Mark to reach a higher level of climax himself.

Finally, she knew that although Ty was someone she would be able to explore her sexuality with, their relationship could never grow beyond that.

Destiny knew that Mark was her soul mate and her love for Mark and his love for her was much deeper than anything she could have with Ty. And for as long as Mark enjoyed sharing her with another man, Destiny knew she would enjoy being shared.

For more info, give feedback and to see other books by Taylor Thomas check-out:

taylor-thomas-2.blogspot.com

Or email:

taylorthomas405@gmail.com

Printed in Great Britain
by Amazon.co.uk, Ltd.,
Marston Gate.